LOUIS L'AMOUR'S GIANT
NOVEL OF THE EARLY WEST

THE DAYBREAKERS

I hunkered in the buffalo wallow,
holding my horse down, because
there's a time for fighting and a time
to run. This time I couldn't run.

There were Indians riding circles out
on the plain, and I knew there were
others crawling closer through the
sagebrush. The horse pricked his ears,
and I turned just in time. Four Utes
were sneaking up the slope in back
of me.

I snapped off a shot –

I had to get out of that buffalo hole
alive, not just for me, but for my
brother Orrin. The frontier was
crawling with men who wanted to kill
Orrin, and he needed me. Me and
my gun.

Louis L'Amour

The Daybreakers

CORGI BOOKS
A DIVISION OF TRANSWORLD PUBLISHERS LTD
A NATIONAL GENERAL COMPANY

THE DAYBREAKERS

A CORGI BOOK 0 552 09112 X

First publication in Great Britain

PRINTING HISTORY
Corgi edition published 1972

Corgi Books are published by
Transworld Publishers Ltd.,
Cavendish House, 57–59 Uxbridge Road,
Ealing, London W.5.
Made and printed in Great Britain
by Cox & Wyman Ltd.,
London, Reading and Fakenham

**NOTE: The Australian price appearing on the
back cover is the recommended retail price.**

Chapter I

MY BROTHER, Orrin Sackett, was big enough to fight bears with a switch. Me, I was the skinny one, tall as Orrin, but no meat to my bones except around the shoulders and arms. Orrin could sing like an angel, or like a true Welshman which was better than any angel. Far away back and on three sides of the family, we were Welsh. Orrin was a strapping big man, but for such a big man he was surprising quick.

Folks said I was the quiet one, and in the high-up hills where we grew up as boys, folks fought shy of me come fighting time. Orrin was bigger than me, fit to wrassle a bull, but he lacked a streak of something I had.

Maybe you recall the Sackett-Higgins feud? Time I tell about, we Sacketts were just fresh out of Higginses.

Long Higgins, the mean one, was also the last one. He came hunting Sackett hide with an old squirrel rifle. It was Orrin he was hunting, being mighty brave because he knew Orrin wouldn't be packing anything in the way of sidearms at a wedding.

Orrin was doing no thinking about Higginses this day with Mary Tripp there to greet him and his mind set on marrying, so I figured it was my place to meet Long Higgins down there in the road. Just as I was fixing to call him to a stand, Preacher Myrick drove his rig between us, and by the time I got around it Long Higgins was standing spraddle-legged in the road with a bead on Orrin.

Folks started to scream and Long Higgins shot and Mary who saw him first pushed Orrin to save him. Only she fell off balance and fell right into the bullet intended for Orrin.

"*Long!*"

1

He turned sharp around, knowing my voice, and he had that rifle waist-high and aimed for me, his lips drawed down hard.

Long Higgins was a good hip shot with a rifle and he shot quick . . . maybe too quick.

That old hog-leg of mine went back into the holster and Long Higgins lay there in the dust and when I turned around, that walk up into the trees was the longest I ever did take except one I took a long time later.

Ollie Shaddock might have been down there and I knew if Ollie called I'd have to turn around, for Ollie was the Law in those mountains and away back somewheres we were kin.

When Ma saw me cutting up through the woods she knew something was cross-ways. Took me only a minute to tell her. She sat in that old rocker and looked me right in the eye while I told it. "Tye," she was almighty stern, "was Long Higgins looking at you when you fetched him?"

"Right in the eye."

"Take the dapple," Ma said, "he's the runningest horse on the mountain. You go west, and when you find a place with deep, rich soil and a mite of game in the hills, you get somebody to write a letter and we'll come down there, the boys an' me."

She looked around at the place, which was mighty run-down. Work as we would, and us Sacketts were workers, we still hadn't anything extra, and scarcely a poor living, so Ma had been talking up the west ever since Pa died.

Most of it she got from Pa, for he was a wandering and a knowing man, never to home long, but Ma loved him for all of that, and so did we younguns. He had a Welshman's tongue, Pa did, a tongue that could twist a fine sound from a word and he could bring a singing to your blood so you could just see that far land yonder, waiting for folks to come and crop it.

Those old blue eyes of Ma's were harder to face than was Long Higgins, and him with a gun to hand. "Tye, do you reckon you could kill Ollie?"

To nobody else would I have said it, but to Ma I told the truth. "I'd never want to, Ma, because we're kin but I could fetch him. I think maybe I can draw a gun faster and shoot straighter than anybody, anywhere."

She took the pipe from her lips. "Eighteen years now I've seen you growing up, Tyrel Sackett, and for twelve of them you've been drawing and shooting. Pa told me when you was fifteen that he'd never seen the like. Ride with the law, Tye, never against it." She drew the shawl tighter about her

2

knees. "If the Lord wills we will meet again in the western lands."

The way I took led across the state line and south, then west. Ollie Shaddock would not follow beyond the line of the state, so I put Tennessee behind me before the hills had a shadow.

It was wild land through which the trail led, west out of Tennessee, into Arkansas, the Ozarks, and by lonely trails into Kansas. When I rode at last into the street at Baxter Springs folks figured me for one more mountain renegade coming to help keep tick-infected Texas cattle out of the country, but I was of no such mind.

It was eight miles to where the Texas men held their cattle, so there I rode, expecting no warm welcome for a stranger. Riding clear of the circling riders I rode up to the fire, the smell of grub turning my insides over. Two days I'd been without eating, with no money left, and too proud to ask for that for which I could not pay.

A short, square man with a square face and a mustache called out to me. "You there! On the gray! What do you want?"

"A job if one's to be had, and a meal if you've grub to spare. My name is Tyrel Sackett and I'm bound westward from Tennessee toward the Rockies, but if there's a job I'll ride straight up to it."

He looked me over, mighty sharp, and then he said, "Get down, man, and come to the fire. No man was ever turned from my fire without a meal inside him. I'm Belden."

When I'd tied Dapple I walked up to the fire, and there was a big, handsome man lying on the ground by the fire, a man with a golden beard like one of those Vikings Pa used to tell of. "Hell," he said agreeably, "it's a farmer!"

"What's wrong with farming?" I asked him. "You wouldn't have your belly full of beans right now if they'd not been farmed by somebody."

"We've had our troubles with farmers, Mr. Sackett," Belden said, "there's been shooting, the farmers killed a man for me."

"So," said a voice alongside, "so maybe we should kill a farmer."

He had an itch for trouble and his kind I'd met before. He was a medium-tall man with a low hanging shoulder on his gun side. His black brows met over his nose and his face was thin and narrow. If it was trouble he was hunting he was following the right trail to get it.

"Mister," I told him, "any time you think you can kill this farmer, you just have at it."

3

He looked across the fire at me, surprised I think, because he had expected fear. My clothes showed I was from the hills, a patched, old homespun shirt, jeans stuffed into clumsy boots. It was sure that I looked like nothing at all, only if a man looked at the pistol I wore he could see there'd been a sight of lead shot out of that barrel.

"That's enough, Carney!" Mr. Belden said sharply. "This man is a guest at our fire!"

The cook brought me a plate of grub and it smelled so good I didn't even look up until I'd emptied that plate and another, and swallowed three cups of hot black coffee. Up in the hills we like our coffee strong but this here would make bobwire grow on a man's chest in the place of hair.

The man with the golden beard watched me and he said to Mr. Belden, "Boss, you better hire this man. If he can work like he can eat, you've got yourself a hand."

"Question is," Carney broke in, "can he fight?"

It was mighty quiet around that fire when I put my plate aside and got up. "Mister, I didn't kill you before because when I left home I promised Ma I'd go careful with a gun, but you're a mighty tryin' man."

Carney had the itch, all right, and as he looked across the fire at me I knew that sooner or later I was going to have to kill this man.

"You promised Ma, did you?" he scoffed. "We'll see about that!" He brought his right foot forward about an inch and I durned near laughed at him, but then from behind me came a warm, rich voice and it spoke clear and plain. "Mister, you just back up an' set down. I ain't aimin' to let Tyrel hang up your hide right now, so you just set down an' cool off."

It was Orrin, and knowing Orrin I knew his rifle covered Carney.

"Thanks, Orrin. Ma made me promise to go careful."

"She told me . . . an' lucky for this gent."

He stepped down from the saddle, a fine, big, handsome man with shoulders wide enough for two strong men. He wore a belt gun, too, and I knew he could use it.

"Are you two brothers?" Belden asked.

"Brothers from the hills," Orrin said, "bound west for the new lands."

"You're hired," Mr. Belden said, "I like men who work together."

So that was how it began, but more had begun that day than any of us could guess, least of all the fine-looking man with the beard who was Tom Sunday, our foreman on the drive. From the moment he had spoken up all our lives were pointed down a trail together, but no man could read the sign.

From the first Orrin was a well-loved man. With that big, easy way of his, a wide smile, as well as courage and humor enough for three men, he was a man to ride the trail with. He did his share of the work and more, and at night around the fire he would sing or tell yarns. When he sang to the cows in that fine Welsh baritone of his, everybody listened.

Nobody paid me much mind. Right off they saw I could do my work and they let me do it. When Orrin told them I was the tough one of the two they just laughed. Only there was one or two of them who didn't laugh and of these one was Tom Sunday, the other Cap Rountree, a thin, wiry old man with a walrus mustache who looked to have ridden a lot of trails.

The third day out, Tom Sunday fetched up alongside me and asked, "Tye, what would you have done if Reed Carney had grabbed his gun?"

"Why, Mr. Sunday," I said, "I'd have killed him."

He glanced at me. "Yes, I expect you would have."

He swung off then, only turned in his saddle. "Call me Tom. I'm not much on long-handled names."

Have you seen those Kansas plains? Have you seen the grass stretch away from you to the horizon? Grass and nothing but grass except for flowers here and there and maybe the white of buffalo bones, but grass moving gentle under the long wind, moving like a restless sea with the hand of God upon it.

On the fifth day when I was riding point by myself, and well out from the herd a dozen men came riding out of a ravine, all bunched up. Right off I had a smell of trouble, so instead of waiting for them to come up, I rode right to meet them.

It was a mighty pleasant day and the air was balmy with summer. Overhead the sky was blue and only a mite of cloud drifting like a lost white buffalo over the plain of the sky.

When they were close I drew up and waited, my Spencer .56 cradled on my saddle, my right hand over the trigger guard.

They drew up, a dirty, rough-looking bunch—their leader mean enough to sour cream.

"We're cuttin' your herd," he was a mighty abrupt man, "we're cuttin' it now. You come through the settlements an' swept up a lot of our cattle, an' they've et our grass."

5

Well, I looked at him and I said, "I reckon not."

Sort of aimlesslike I'd switched that Spencer to cover his belt buckle, my right finger on the trigger.

"Look here, boy," he started in to bluster.

"Mister," I said, "this here Spencer ain't no boy, an' I'm just after makin' a bet with a fellow. He says one of those big belt buckles like you got would stop a bullet. Me, I figure a chunk of lead, .56 caliber would drive that buckle right back into your belly. Mister, if you want to be a sport we can settle that bet."

He was white around the eyes, and if one of the others made a wrong move I was going to drop the bull of the herd and as many others as time would allow.

"Back," it was one of the men behind the leader, "I know this boy. This here is one of them Sacketts I been tellin' you about."

It was one of those no-account Aikens from Turkey Flat, who'd been run out of the mountains for hog stealing.

"Oh?" Back smiled, kind of sickly. "Had no idea you was friends. Boy," he said, "you folks just ride on through."

"Thanks. That there's just what we figured to do."

They turned tail around and rode off and a couple of minutes later hoofs drummed on the sod and here came Mr. Belden, Tom Sunday, Cap Rountree, and Reed Carney, all a-sweat an' expecting trouble. When they saw those herd cutters ride off they were mighty surprised.

"Tye," Mr. Belden asked, "what did those men want?"

"They figured to cut your herd."

"What happened?"

"They decided not to."

He looked at me, mighty sharp. Kneeing Dapple around I started back to the herd.

"Now what do you make of that?" I could hear Belden saying. "I'd have sworn that was Back Rand."

"It was," Rountree commented dryly, "but that there's quite a boy."

When Orrin asked me about it at fire that night, I just said, "Aiken was there. From Turkey Flat."

Carney was listening. "Aiken who? Who's Aiken?"

"He's from the mountains," Orrin said, "he knows the kid."

Reed Carney said nothing more but a couple of times I noticed him sizing me up like he hadn't seen me before.

There would be trouble enough, but man is born to trouble, and it is best to meet it when it comes and not lose sleep until it does. Only there was more than trouble, for beyond the long grass plains were the mountains, the high and lone-

ly mountains where someday I would ride, and where someday, the Good Lord willing, I would find a home.

How many trails? How much dust and loneliness? How
long a time until then?

Chapter II

THERE WAS nothing but prairie and sky, the sun by day
and the stars by night, and the cattle moving westward. If
I live to be a thousand years old I shall not forget the wonder and the beauty of those big longhorns, the sun glinting
on their horns; most of them six or seven feet from tip to
tip. Some there were like old brindle, our lead steer, whose
horns measured a fair nine feet from point to point, and who
stood near to seventeen hands high.

It was a sea of horns above the red, brown, brindle, and
white-splashed backs of the steers. They were big, wild, and
fierce, ready to fight anything that walked the earth, and we
who rode their flanks or the drag, we loved them and we
hated them, we cussed and reviled them, but we moved them
westward toward what destination we knew not.

Sometimes at night when my horse walked a slow circle
around the bedded herd, I'd look at the stars and think of Ma
and wonder how things were at home. And sometimes I'd
dream great dreams of a girl I'd know someday.

Suddenly something had happened to me, and it happened
to Orrin too. The world had burst wide open, and where
our narrow valleys had been, our hog-backed ridges, our
huddled towns and villages, there was now a world without
end or limit. Where our world had been one of a few mountain valleys, it was now as wide as the earth itself, and
wider, for where the land ended there was sky, and no end at
all to that.

We saw no one. The Plains were empty. No cattle had
been before us, only the buffalo and war parties of Indians
crossing. No trees, only the far and endless grass, always
whispering its own soft stories. Here ran the antelope, and by
night the coyotes called their plaintive songs to the silent
stars.

Mostly a man rode by himself, but sometimes I'd ride along
with Tom Sunday or Cap Rountree, and I learned about cattle
from them. Sunday knew cows, all right, but he was a sight

better educated than the rest of us, although not one for showing it.

Sometimes when we rode along he would recite poetry or tell me stories from the history of ancient times, and it was mighty rich stuff. Those old Greeks he was always talking about, they reminded me of mountain folk I'd known, and it fair made me ache to know how to read myself.

Rountree talked mighty little, but whatever he said made a sight of sense. He knew buffalo . . . although there was always something to learn about them. He was a mighty hard old man, rode as many hours as any of us, although he was a mighty lot older. I never did know how old he was, but those hard old gray eyes of his had looked on a sight of strange things.

"Man could make some money," Rountree said one day, "over in the breaks of western Kansas and Colorado. Lots of cows over there, belongin' to nobody, stuff drifted up from the Spanish settlements to the south."

When Rountree spoke up it was because there was an idea behind it. Right then I figured something was stirring in that coot's skull, but nothing more was said at the time.

Orrin and me, we talked it over. Each of us wanted a place of our own, and we wanted a place for Ma and the boys. A lot of cattle belonging to no man . . . it sounded good to us.

"It would take an outfit," Orrin said.

Tom Sunday, I was sure, would be for it. From things he'd said on night herd I knew he was an ambitious man, and he had plans for himself out west. Educated the way he was, there was no telling how far he would go. Time to time he talked a good deal about politics . . . out west a man could be whatever he was man enough to be, and Tom Sunday was smart.

"Orrin and me," I said to Rountree, "we've been talking about what you said. About those wild cows. We discussed the three of us and maybe Tom Sunday, if you're willing and he wants to come in."

"Why, now. That there's about what I had in mind. Fact is, I talked to Tom. He likes it."

Mr. Belden drove his herd away from the Kansas-Missouri border, right out into the grassy plains, he figured he'd let his cows graze until they were good and fat, then sell them in Abilene; there were cattle buyers buying and shipping cattle from there because of the railroad.

Anybody expecting Abilene to be a metropolis would have been some put out, but to Orrin and me, who had never seen anything bigger than Baxter Springs, it looked right smart of a town. Why, Abilene was quite a place, even if you did have to look mighty fast to see what there was of it.

Main thing was that railroad. I'd heard tell of railroads before, but had never come right up to one. Wasn't much to see: just two rails of steel running off into the distance, bedded down on crossties of hewn logs. There were some stock pens built there and about a dozen log houses. There was a saloon in a log house, and across the tracks there was a spanking-new hotel three stories high with a porch along the side fronting the rails. Folks had told me there were buildings that tall, but I never figured to see one.

There was another hotel, too. Placed called Bratton's, with six rooms to let. East of the hotel there was a saloon run by a fat man called Jones. There was a stage station . . . that was two stories . . . a blacksmith shop and the Frontier Store.

At the Drovers' Cottage there was a woman cooking there and some rooms were let, and there were three, four cattle buyers loafing around.

We bunched our cows on the grass outside of town and Mr. Belden rode in to see if he could make a deal, although he didn't much like the look of things. Abilene was too new, it looked like a put-up job and Kansas hadn't shown us no welcome signs up to now.

Then Mr. Belden came back and durned if he hadn't hired several men to guard the herd so's we could have a night in town . . . not that she was much of a place, like I said. But we went in.

Orrin and me rode down alongside the track, and Orrin was singing in that big, fine-sounding voice of his, and when we came abreast of the Drovers' Cottage there was a girl a-setting on the porch.

She had a kind of pale blond hair and skin like it never saw daylight, and blue eyes that made a man think she was the prettiest thing he ever did see. Only second glance she reminded me somehow of a hammer-headed roan we used to have, the one with the one blue eye . . . a mighty ornery horse, too narrow between the ears and eyes. On that second glance I figured that blonde had more than a passing likeness to that bronc.

But when she looked at Orrin I knew we were in for trouble, for if ever I saw a man-catching look in a woman's eyes it was in hers, then.

"Orrin," I said, "if you want to run maverick a few more years, if you want to find that western land, then you stay off that porch."

"Boy," he put a big hand on my shoulder, "look at that yaller hair!"

"Reminds me of that hammer-headed, no-account roan we used to have. Pa he used to say, 'size up a woman the way you would a horse if you were in a horse trade; and Orrin, you better remember that."

Orrin laughed. "Stand aside, youngster," he tells me, "and watch how it's done."

With that Orrin rides right up to the porch and standing up in his stirrups he said, "Howdy, ma'am! A mighty fine evening! Might I come up an' set with you a spell?"

Mayhap he needed a shave and a bath like we all did, but there was something in him that always made a woman stop and look twice.

Before she could answer a tall man stepped out. "Young man," he spoke mighty sharp, "I will thank you not to annoy my daughter. She does not consort with hired hands."

Orrin smiled that big, wide smile of his. "Sorry, sir, I did not mean to offend. I was riding by, and such beauty, sir, such beauty deserves its tribute, sir."

Then he flashed that girl a smile, then reined his horse around and we rode on to the saloon.

The saloon wasn't much, but it took little to please us. There was about ten feet of bar, sawdust on the floor, and not more than a half-dozen bottles behind the bar. There was a barrel of mighty poor whiskey. Any farmer back in our country could make better whiskey out of branch water and corn, but we had our drinks and then Orrin and me hunted the barrels out back.

Those days, in a lot of places a man might get to, barrels were the only place a man could bathe. You stripped off and you got into a barrel and somebody poured water over you, then after soaping down and washing as best you could you'd have more water to rinse off the soap, and you'd had yourself a bath.

"You watch yo'se'f," the saloon keeper warned, "feller out there yestiddy shot himself a rattler whilst he was in the barrel."

Orrin bathed in one barrel, Tom Sunday in another, while I shaved in a piece of broken mirror tacked to the back wall of the saloon. When they finished bathing I stripped off and got into the barrel and Orrin and Tom, they took off. Just when I was wet all over, Reed Carney came out of the saloon.

My gun was close by but my shirt had fallen over it and there was no chance to get a hand on it in a hurry.

So there I was, naked as a jaybird, standing in a barrel two-thirds full of water, and there was that trouble-hunting Reed Carney with two or three drinks under his belt and a grudge under his hat.

It was my move, but it had to be the right move at the right time, and to reach for that gun would be the wrong thing to do. Somehow I had to get out of that tub and there I was with soap all over me, in my hair and on my face and dribbling toward my eyes.

The rinse water was in a bucket close to the barrel so acting mighty unconcerned I reached down, picked it up, sloshing it over me to wash off that soap.

"Orrin," Carney said, grinning at me, "went to the *ho*-tel and it don't seem hardly right, you in trouble and him not here to stand in front of you."

"Orrin handles his business. I handle mine."

He walked up to within three or four feet of the barrel and there was something in his eyes I'd not seen before. I knew then he meant to kill me.

"I've been wonderin' about that. I'm curious to see if you can handle your own affairs without that big brother standing by to pull you out."

The bucket was still about a third full of water and I lifted it to slash it over me.

There was a kind of nasty, wet look to his eyes and he took a step nearer. "I don't like you," he said, "and I—" His hand dropped to his gun and I let him have the rest of that water in the face.

He jumped back and I half-jumped, half-fell out of the barrel just as he blinked the water away and grabbed iron. His gun was coming up when the bucket's edge caught him alongside the skull and I felt the *whiff* of that bullet past my ear. But that bucket was oak and it was heavy and it laid him out cold.

Inside the saloon there was a scramble of boots, and picking up the flour-sack towel I began drying off, but I was standing right beside my gun and I had the shirt pulled away from it and easy to my hand it was. If any friends of Carney's wanted to call the tune I was ready for the dance.

The first man out was a tall, blond man with a narrow, tough face and a twisted look to his mouth caused by an old scar. He wore his gun tied to his leg and low down the way some of these fancy gunmen wear them. Cap Rountree was only a step behind and right off he pulled over to one side and hung a hand near his gun butt. Tom Sunday fanned out on the other side. Two others ranged up along the man with the scarred lip.

"What happened?"

"Carney here," I said, "bought himself more than he could pay for."

That blond puncher had been ready to buy himself a piece

11

of any fight there was left and he was just squaring away when Cap Rountree put in his two-bit's worth. "We figured you might be troubled, Tye," Cap said in that dry, hard old voice, "so Tom an' me, we came out to see the sides were even up."

You could feel the change in the air. That blond with the scarred lip—later I found out his name was Fetterson—he didn't like the situation even a little. Here I was dead center in front of him, but he and his two partners, they were framed by Tom Sunday and Cap Rountree.

Fetterson glanced one way and then the other and you could just see his horns pull in. He'd come through that door sure enough on the prod an' pawin' dust, but suddenly he was so peaceful it worried me.

"You better hunt yourself a hole before he comes out of it," Fetterson said. "He'll stretch your hide."

By that time I had my pants on and was stamping into my boots. Believe me, I sure hate to face up to trouble with no pants on, and no boots.

So I slung my gun belt and settled my holster into place. "You tell him to draw his pay and rattle his hocks out of here. I ain't hunting trouble, but he's pushing, mighty pushing."

The three of us walked across to the Drovers' Cottage for a meal, and the first thing we saw was Orrin setting down close to that blond girl and she was looking at him like he was money from home. But that was the least of it. Her father was setting there listening himself . . . leave it to Orrin and that Welsh-talking tongue of his. He could talk a squirrel right out of a walnut tree . . . I never saw the like.

The three of us sat down to a good meal and we talked up a storm about that country to the west, and the wild cattle, and how much a man could make if he could keep Comanches, Kiowas, or Utes from lifting his hair.

Seemed strange to be sitting at a table. We were all so used to setting on the ground that we felt awkward with a white cloth and all. Out on the range a man ate with his hunting knife and what he could swab up with a chunk of bread.

That night Mr. Belden paid us off in the hotel office, and one by one we stepped up for our money. You've got to remember that neither Orrin or me had ever had twenty-five dollars of cash money in our lives before. In the mountains a man mostly swapped for what he needed, and clothes were homespun.

Our wages were twenty-five dollars a month and Orrin and me had two months and part of a third coming.

Only when he came to me, Mr. Belden put down his pen and sat back in his chair.

"Tye," he said, "there's a prisoner here who is being held for the United States Marshal. Brought in this morning. His name is Aiken, and he was riding with Back Rand the day you met them out on the prairie."

"Yes, sir."

"I had a talk with Aiken, and he told me that if it hadn't been for you Back Rand would have taken my herd . . or tried to. It seems, from what he said, that you saved my herd or saved us a nasty fight and a stampede where I was sure to lose cattle. It seems this Aiken knew all about you Sacketts and he told Rand enough so that Rand didn't want to call your bluff. I'm not an ungrateful man, Tye, so I'm adding two hundred dollars to your wages."

Two hundred dollars was a sight of money, those days, cash money being a shy thing.

When we walked out on the porch of the Drovers' Cottage, there were three wagons coming up the trail, and three more behind them. The first three were army ambulances surrounded by a dozen Mexicans in fringed buckskin suits and wide Mexican sombreros. There were another dozen riding around the three freight wagons following, and we'd never seen the like.

Their jackets were short, only to the waist, and their pants flared out at the bottom and fitted like a glove along the thighs. Their spurs had rowels like mill wheels on them, and they all had spanking-new rifles and pistols. They wore colored silk sashes like some of those Texas cowhands wore, and they were all slicked out like some kind of a show.

Horses? Mister, you should see such horses! Every one clean-limbed and quick, and every one showing he'd been curried and fussed over. Every man Jack of that crowd was well set-up, and if ever I saw a fighting crowd, it was this lot.

The first carriage drew up before the Drovers' Cottage and a tall, fine-looking old man with pure white hair and white mustaches got down from the wagon, then helped a girl down. Now I couldn't rightly say how old she was, not being any judge of years on a woman, but I'd guess she was fifteen or sixteen, and the prettiest thing I ever put an eye to.

Pa had told us a time or two about those Spanish *dons* and the *señoritas* who lived around Santa Fe, and these folks must be heading that direction.

Right then I had me an idea. In Indian country the more rifles the better, and this here outfit must muster forty rifles if there was one, and no Indian was going to tackle that bunch for the small amount of loot those wagons promised.

13

The four of us would make their party that much stronger, and would put us right in the country we were headed for.

Saying nothing to Sunday or Rountree, I went into the dining room. The grub there was passing fine. Situated on the rails they could get about what they wanted and the Drovers' Cottage was all set up to cater to cattlemen and cattle buyers with money to spend. Later on folks from back east told me some of the finest meals they ever set down to were in some of those western hotels . . . and some of the worst, too.

The don was sitting at a table with that pretty girl, but right away I could see this was no setup to buck if a man was hunting trouble. There were buckskin-clad riders setting at tables around them and when I approached the don, four of them came out of their chairs like they had springs in their pants, and they stood as if awaiting a signal.

"Sir," I said, "from the look of your outfit you'll be headed for Santa Fe. My partners and me . . . there are four of us . . . we're headed west. If we could ride along with your party we'd add four rifles to your strength and it would be safer for us."

He looked at me out of cold eyes from a still face. His mustache was beautifully white, his skin a pale tan, his eyes brown and steady. He started to speak, but the girl interrupted and seemed to be explaining something to him, but there was no doubt about his answer.

She looked up at me. "I am sorry, sir, but my grandfather says it will be impossible."

"I'm sorry, too," I said, "but if he would like to check up on our character he could ask Mr. Belden over there."

She explained, and the old man glanced at Mr. Belden across the room. There was a moment when I thought he might change his mind, but he shook his head.

"I am sorry." She looked like she really was sorry. "My grandfather is a very positive man." She hesitated and then she said, "We have been warned that we may be attacked by some of your people."

I bowed . . . more than likely it was mighty awkward, it was the first time I ever bowed to anybody, but it seemed the thing to do.

"My name is Tyrel Sackett, and if ever we can be of help, my friends and I are at your service." I meant it, too, although that speech was right out a book I'd heard read one time, and it made quite an impression on me. "I mean, I'll sure come a-foggin' it if you're in trouble."

She smiled at me, mighty pretty, and I turned away from that table with my head whirling like somebody had hit me with a whiffletree.

Orrin had come in, and he was setting up to a table with that blond girl and her father, but the way those two glared at me you'd have sworn I'd robbed a hen roost.

Coming down off the steps I got a glimpse into that wagon the girl had been riding in. You never seen the like. It was all plush and pretty, fixed up like nothing you ever saw, a regular little room for her. The second wagon was the old man's, and later I learned that the third carted supplies for them, fine food and such, with extra rifles, ammunition, and clothing. The three freight wagons were heavy-loaded for their rancho in New Mexico.

Orrin followed me outside. "How'd you get to know Don Luis?"

"That his name? I just up an' talked to him."

"Pritts tells me he's not well thought of by his neighbors." Orrin lowered his voice. "Fact is, Tyrel, they're getting an outfit together to drive him out."

"Is that Pritts? That feller you've been talking to?"

"Jonathan Pritts and his daughter Laura. Mighty fine New England people. He's a town-site developer. She wasn't pleased to come west and leave their fine home behind and all their fine friends, but her Pa felt it his duty to come west and open up the country for the right people."

Now something about that didn't sound right to me, nor did it sound like Orrin. Remembering how my own skull was buzzing over that Spanish girl I figured he must have it the same way over that narrow-between-the-eyes blond girl.

"Seems to me, Orrin, that most folks don't leave home unless they figure to gain by it. We are going west because we can't make a living out of no side-hill farm. I reckon you'll find Jonathan Pritts ain't much different."

Orrin was shocked. "Oh, no. Nothing like that. He was a big man where he came from. If he had stayed there he would be running for the Senate right now."

"Seems to me," I said, "that somebody has told you a mighty lot about her fine friends and her fine home. If he does any developin' it won't be from goodness of his heart but because there's money to be had."

"You don't understand, Tyrel. These are fine people. You should get acquainted."

"We'll have little time for people out west rounding up cows."

Orrin looked mighty uncomfortable. "Mr. Pritts has offered me a job, running his outfit. Plans to develop town sites and the like; there's a lot of old Spanish grants that will be opened to settlement."

"He's got some men?"

"A dozen now, more later. I met one of them, Fetterson."

"With a scarred lip?"

"Why, sure!" Orrin looked at me mighty curious. "Do you know him?"

For the first time then I told Orrin about the shindig back of the saloon when I belted Reed Carney with the bucket.

"Why, then," Orrin said quietly, "I won't take the job. I'll tell Mr. Pritts about Fetterson, too." He paused. "Although I'd like to keep track of Laura."

"Since when have you started chasing girls? Seems to me they always chased after you."

"Laura's different . . . I never knew a city girl before, and she's mighty fine. Manners and all." Right then it seemed to me that if he never saw them again it would be too soon . . . all those fancy city manners and city fixings had turned Orrin's head.

Another thing. Jonathan Pritts was talking about those Spanish land grants that would be opened to settlement. It set me to wondering just what would happen to those Spanish folks who owned the grants?

Sizing up those riders of the don's I figured no rawhide outfit made up of the likes of Fetterson would have much chance shaking the don's loose from their land. But that was no business of ours. Starting tomorrow we were wild-cow hunters.

Anyway, Orrin was six years older than me and he had always had luck with girls and no girl ever paid me much mind, so I was sure in no position to tell him.

This Laura Pritts was a pretty thing . . . no taking that away from her. Nonetheless I couldn't get that contrary hammerheaded roan out of mind. They surely did favor.

Orrin had gone back into the cottage and I walked to the edge of the street. Several of the don's riders were loafing near their wagons and it was mighty quiet.

Rountree spoke from the street. "Watch yourself, Tye."

Turning, I looked around.

Reed Carney was coming up the street.

Chapter III

BACK in the hills Orrin was the well-liked brother, nor did I ever begrudge him that. Not that folks disliked me or that I ever went around being mean, but folks never did get close to me and it was most likely my fault. There was always something standoffish about me. I liked folks, but I liked the wild animals, the lonely trails, and the mountains better.

Pa told me once, "Tyrel, you're different. Don't you ever regret it. Folks won't cotton to you much, but the friends you will make will be good friends and they'll stand by you."

Those days I thought he was wrong. I never felt any different than anybody else, far as I could see, only now when I saw Reed Carney coming up the street, and knowing it was me he was coming to kill, something came up in me that I'd never felt before, not even when Long Higgins started for Orrin.

It was something fierce and terrible that came up and liked to choke me, and then it was gone and I was very quiet inside. The moments seemed to plod, every detail stood out in sharp focus, clear and strong. Every sense, every emotion was caught and held, concentrated on that man coming up the street.

He was not alone.

Fetterson was with him, and the two who had come from the saloon when I laid Carney low with the bucket. They were a little behind him and spread out.

Orrin was inside somewhere and only that dry, harsh old man with his wolf eyes was there. He would know what was to be done, for nobody needed to tell him how to play his cards in a situation like this . . . and no one needed to tell me. Suddenly, with a queer wave of sadness and fatality, I realized that it was for moments such as this that I had been born.

Some men are gifted to paint, some to write, and some to lead men. For me it was always to be this, not to kill men, although in the years to come I was to kill more than I liked, but to command such situations as this.

Reed was coming up the street and he was thinking what folks would say when they told the story in the cow camps and around the chuck wagons. He was thinking of how they would tell of him walking up the street to kill Tyrel Sackett.

Me, I wasn't thinking. I was just standing there. I was just me, and I knew some things were inevitable.

On my right a door closed and I knew Don Luis had come out on the porch. I even heard, it was that still, the scratch of the match when he lit his cigar.

When Reed started at me he was more than a hundred yards off, but when he had covered half the distance, I started to meet him.

He stopped.

Seems like he didn't expect me to come hunting it. Seems

like he figured he was the hunter and that I would try to avoid a shoot out. Seems like something had happened to him in that fifty yards, for fifty yards can be a lifetime.

Suddenly, I knew I didn't have to kill him. Mayhap that was the moment when I changed from a boy into a man. Somewhere I'd begun to learn things about myself and about gunfights and gunfighters. Reading men is the biggest part; drawing fast, even shooting straight, they come later. And some of the fastest drawing men with guns were among the first to die. That fast draw didn't mean a thing . . . not a thing.

The first thing I was learning was there are times when a man had to kill and times when he had no need to.

Reed Carney wanted a shoot out and he wanted to win, but me, I'm more than average contrary.

Watching Reed come up the street, I knew I didn't need a gun for him; suddenly it came over me that Reed Carney was nothing but a tinhorn. He fancied himself as a tough man and a gunfighter, but he didn't really want anybody shooting at him. The trouble with having a reputation as a tough man is that the time always comes when you have to be a tough man. It's a whole lot different.

Nothing exciting or thrilling about a gunfight. She's a mighty cold proposition for both parties. One or t'other is to be killed or hurt bad, maybe both.

Some folks take chances because they've got it in their minds they're somebody special, that something will protect them. It is always, they figure, somebody else who dies.

Only it ain't thataway. *You* can die. You can be snuffed out like you never existed at all and a few minutes after you're buried nobody will care except maybe your wife or your mother. You stick your finger in the water and you pull it out, and that's how much of a hole you leave when you're gone.

Reed Carney had been thinking of himself as a mighty dangerous man and he had talked himself into a shoot out.

Maybe it was something in his walk or the way he looked or in the fact that he stopped when I started toward him. Mayhap it was something sensed rather than seen, that something within me that made me different than other men. Only suddenly I knew that by the time he had taken ten steps toward me the fight had begun to peter out of him, that for the first time he was realizing that I was going to be shooting at him to kill.

Panic can hit a man. You never really know. You can have a man bluffed and then something wild hits him and you're in a real honest-to-warchief shooting.

Those others were going to wait for Reed, but I'd leave them to Cap. Reed was my problem and I knew he wanted to kill me. Or rather, he wanted it known around that he'd killed me.

As I walked toward him I knew Reed knew he should draw, and he felt sure he was going to draw, but he just stood there. Then he knew that if he didn't draw it would be too late.

The sweat was streaming down his cheeks although it wasn't a hot evening. Only I just kept walking up on him, closing in. He took a step back and his lips parted like he was having trouble breathing, and he knew that if he didn't draw on me then he would never be the same man again as long as he lived.

When I stopped I was within arm's length of him and he was breathing like he'd run a long way uphill.

"I'd kill you, Reed."

It was the first time I'd ever called him by his first name and his eyes looked right into mine, startled, like a youngster's.

"You want to be a big man, Reed, but you'll never make it with a gun. You just ain't trimmed right for it. If you'd moved for that gun you'd be dead now . . . cold and dead in the dust down there with only the memory of a gnawing rat of pain in your belly.

"Now you reach down mighty careful, Reed, and you unbuckle your belt and let it fall. Then you turn around and walk away."

It was still. A tiny puff of wind stirred dust, then died out. Somewhere on the porch of the Drovers' Cottage a board creaked as somebody shifted weight. Out on the prairie a meadow lark sang.

"Unbuckle the belt!"

His eyes were fastened on mine, large and open. Sweat trickled down his cheeks in rivulets. His tongue fumbled at his lips and then his fingers reached for his belt buckle. As he let the belt fall there was a gasp from somewhere, and for a split second everything hung by a hair. There was a moment then when he might have grabbed for a gun but my eyes had him and he let the belt go.

"Was I you I'd straddle my bronc and light a shuck out of here. You got lots of country to choose from."

He backed off, then turned and started to walk away, and then as he realized what he'd done he walked faster and faster. He stumbled once, caught himself, and kept going.

After a moment I scooped up the gun belt with my left hand and turned back toward the Drovers' Cottage.

They were all on the porch. Orrin, Laura Pritts and her Pa, and Don Luis . . . even his granddaughter.

Fetterson stood there, mad clear through. He had come itching for trouble and he was stopped cold. He had no mind to tackle Cap Rountree for fun . . . nobody wanted any part of that old wolf. But he had a look in those gun-metal eyes of his that would frighten a body.

"I'll buy the drinks," I said.

"Just coffee for me," Cap replied.

My eyes were on Fetterson. "That includes you," I said.

He started to say something mean, and then he said, "Be damned if I won't. That took guts, mister."

Don Luis took the cigar from his lips and brushed away the long ash that had collected there during the moments just past. He looked at me and spoke in Spanish.

"He says we can travel west with him if we like," Cap translated, "he says you are a brave man . . . and what is more important, a wise one."

"*Gracias*," I said, and it was about the only Spanish word I knew.

In 1867, the Santa Fe Trail was an old trail, cut deep with the ruts of the heavy wagons carrying freight over the trail from Independence, Missouri. It was no road, only a wide area whose many ruts showed the way the wagons had gone through the fifty-odd years the trail had been used. Cap Rountree had come over it first in 1836, he said.

Orrin and me, we had an ache inside us for new country, and a longing to see the mountains show up on the horizon.

We had to find a place for Ma, and if we had luck out west, then we could start looking for a place.

Back home we had two younger brothers and one older, but it had been a long time since we'd seen Tell, the oldest of our brothers who was still alive and should be coming home from the wars soon. When the War between the States started he joined up and then stayed on to fight the Sioux in the Dakotas.

We rode west. Of a night we camped together and it sure was fine to set around the fire and listen to those Spanish men sing, and they did a lot of it, one time or another.

Meantime I was listening to Rountree. That old man had learned a lot in his lifetime, living with the Sioux like he did, and with the Nez Perce. First off he taught me to say that name right, and he said it *Nay-Persay*. He taught me a lot about their customs, how they lived, and told me all about those fine horses they raised, the appaloosas.

My clothes had give out so I bought me an outfit from

one of the Spanish men, so I was all fixed out like they were, in a buckskin suit with fringe and all. In the three months since I'd left home I'd put on nearly fifteen pounds and all of it muscle. I sure wished Ma could see me. Only thing that was the same was my gun.

The first few days out I'd seen nothing of the don or his granddaughter, except once when I dropped an antelope with a running shot at three hundred yards. The don happened to see that and spoke of it ...

Sometimes his granddaughter would mount her horse and ride alongside the wagons, and one day when we'd been out for about a week, she cantered up on a ridge where I was looking over the country ahead of us.

A man couldn't take anything for safe in this country. From the top of a low hill that country was open grass as far as you could see. There might be a half-dozen shallow valleys out there or ditches, there might be a canyon or a hollow, and any one of them might be chock full of Indians.

This time that Spanish girl joined me on the ridge, I was sizing up the country. She had beautiful big dark eyes and long lashes and she was about the prettiest thing I ever did see.

"Do you mind if I ride with you, Mr. Sackett?"

"I sure don't mind, but what about Don Luis? I don't expect he'd like his granddaughter riding with a Tennessee drifter."

"He said I could come, but that I must ask your permission. He said you would not let me ride with you if it was not safe."

On the hill where we sat the wind was cool and there was no dust. The train of wagons and pack horses was a half mile away to the southeast. The first Spanish I learned I started learning that day from her.

"Are you going to Santa Fe?"

"No, ma'am, we're going wild-cow hunting along the Purgatoire."

Her name it turned out was Drusilla, and her grandmother had been Irish. The *vaqueros* were not Mexicans but Basques, and like I'd figured, they were picked fighting men. There was always a *vaquero* close by as we rode in case of trouble.

After that first time Drusilla often rode with me, and I noticed the *vaqueros* were watching their back trail as carefully as they watched out for Indians, and some times five or six of them would take off and ride back along the way we had come.

"Grandfather thinks we may be followed and attacked. He has been warned."

That made me think of what Jonathan Pritts had told Orrin, and not knowing if it mattered or not, I told her to tell the don. It seemed to me that land that had been granted a family long ago belonged to that family, and no latecomer like Pritts had a right to move in and drive them off.

The next day she thanked me for her grandfather. Jonathan Pritts had been to Santa Fe before this, and he was working through political means to get their grant revoked so the land could be thrown open to settlement.

Rountree was restless. "By this time we should have met up with Injuns. Keep those rides closer in, Tye, d' you hear?"

He rode in silence for a few minutes, then he said, "Folks back east do a sight of talkin' about the noble red man. Well, he's a mighty fine fighter, I give him that, but ain't no Indian, unless a Nez Perce, who wouldn't ride a couple hundred miles for a fight. Folks talk about takin' land from the Indians. No Indian ever *owned* land, no way. He hunted over the country and he was always fightin' other Indians just for the right to hunt there.

"I fought Injuns and I lived with Injuns. If you walked into an Injun village of your own will they'd feed you an' let you be as long as you stayed . . . that was their way, but the same Injun in whose tipi you slept might follow you when you left an' murder you.

"They hadn't the same upbringin' a white man has. There was none of this talk of mercy, kindness and suchlike which we get from the time we're youngsters. We get it even though most folks don't foller the teachin'. An Injun is loyal to nobody but his own tribe . . . an' any stranger is apt to be an enemy.

"You fight an Injun an' whup him, after that maybe you can trade with him. He'll deal with a fightin' man, but a man who can't protect hisself, well, most Injuns have no respect for him, so they just kill him an' forget him."

Around the fires at night there was talk and laughter. Orrin sang his old Welsh and Irish ballads for them. From Pa he'd picked up some Spanish songs, and when he sang them you should have heard them Spanish men yell! And from the far hills the coyotes answered.

Old Rountree would find a spot well back from the flames and set there watching the outer darkness and listening. A man who stares into flames is blind when he looks into outer darkness, and he won't shoot straight . . . Pa had taught us that, back in Tennessee.

This was Indian country and you have to figure, understanding Indians, that his whole standing in this tribe comes from how many coups he's counted, which means to strike an enemy, a living enemy, or to be the first one to strike a man who has fallen . . . they figure that mighty daring because the fallen man may be playing possum.

An Indian who was a good horse thief, he could have the pick of the girls in the tribe. Mostly because marriage was on the barter system, and an Indian could have all the wives he could afford to buy . . . usually that wasn't more than two or three, and mostly one.

Orrin hadn't forgotten that Laura girl. He was upset with me, too, for leading him off again when he was half a mind to tie up with Pritts.

"He's paying top wages," Orrin said, one night.

"Fighting wages," I said.

"Could be, Tyrel," Orrin said, and no friendly sound to his voice, "that you're holding something against Mr. Pritts. And against Laura, too."

Go easy, boy, I told myself, this is dangerous ground. "I don't know them. Only from what you've said he's planning to horn in on land that doesn't belong to him."

Orrin started to speak but Tom Sunday got up. "Time to turn in," he spoke abruptly, "gettin'-up time comes early."

We turned in, both of us with words we were itching to say that were better unsaid.

It rankled, however. There was truth about me having a holding against Pritts and his daughter. That I had . . . she didn't look right to me, and I've always been suspicious of those too-sanctimonious men like Jonathan Pritts.

The way he looked down that thin New England nose of his didn't promise any good for those who didn't agree with him. And what I said to Orrin that time, I'd believed. If Pritts had been so much back home, what was he doing out here?

We filled our canteens at daybreak with no certain water ahead of us. A hot wind searched the grass. At Mud Creek there was enough water in the creek bottom for the horses, but when we left it it was bone dry. It was seven miles to the Water Holes, and if there was no water there it was a dry day's travel to the Little Arkansas.

The sun was hot. Dust lifted from the feet of the horses and mules, and we left a trail of dust in the air. If any Indians were around, they'd not miss us.

"A man would have to prime himself to spit in country

like this," Tom Sunday remarked. "How about the country we're heading toward, Cap?"

"Worse . . . unless a man knows the land. Only saving thing, there's no travel up thataway except for Comanches. What water there is we'll likely have to ourselves."

Every day then, Drusilla was riding with me. And every day I felt myself looking for her sooner than before. Sometimes we were only out for a half hour, at most an hour, but I got so I welcomed her coming and dreaded her going.

Back in the mountains I'd known few girls. Mostly I fought shy of them, not figuring to put my neck in any loops I couldn't pull out of . . . only I had a feeling I was getting bogged down with Drusilla.

She was shy of sixteen, but Spanish girls marry that young and younger, and in the mountains they did also. Me, I had nothing but a dapple horse, a partnership in some mules, and my old Spencer and a Colt pistol. It didn't count up to much.

Meanwhile, I'd been getting to know the *vaqueros*. I'd never known anybody before who wasn't straight-out American, and back in the hills we held ourselves suspicious of such folk. Riding with them, I was finding they were good, solid men.

Miguel was a slim, wiry man who was the finest rider I ever knew, and maybe a couple of years older than me. He was a handsome man with a quick laugh, and like me he was always ready to ride far afield.

Juan Torres was the boss of the lot, a compact man of forty-three or four, who rarely smiled but was always friendly. Maybe he was the finest rifle shot I ever saw . . . he had worked for Don Luis Alvarado since he, Torres, was a boy, and thought of him like he was a god.

There was Pete Romero, and a slim, tough young devil called Antonio Baca . . . the only one who didn't have the Basque blood. It seemed to me he thought he was a better man than Torres, and there was something else I figured was just my thinking until Cap mentioned it.

"Did you ever notice how young Baca looks at you when you ride with the *señorita?*"

"He doesn't seem to like it. I noticed that."

"You watch yourself. That boy's got a streak of meanness."

That was all Cap said, but I took it to mind. Stories I'd heard made out these Spanish men to be mighty jealous, although no girl was going to look serious at me when there were men around like Orrin and Tom Sunday.

There's no accounting for the notions men get, and it

24

seems to me the most serious trouble between men comes not so much from money, horses, or women, but from notions. A man takes a dislike to another man for no reason at all but that they rub each other wrong, and then something, a horse or a woman or a drink sets it off and they go to shooting or cutting or walloping with sticks.

Like Reed Carney. Only a notion. And it could have got him killed.

At the Little Arkansas we camped where a little branch flowed from a spring in the bluff and ran down to the river. It was good water, maybe a mite brackish.

After night guard was set I slipped out of camp with a rifle and canteen and went down to the Little Arkansas. Dark was coming on but a man could see. Moving down to the river's edge . . . there was more sand than water . . . I stood listening.

A man should trust his senses and they'll grow sharper from use. I never took it for granted that the country was safe. Not only listening and watching as I moved, but testing the air for smells. Out on the prairie where the air is fresh a man can smell more than around people, and after awhile he learns to smell an Indian, a white man, a horse, or even a bear.

Off in the distance there was heat lightning, and a far-off rumble of thunder.

Waiting in the silence after the thunder a stone rattled across the river and a column of riders emerged from the brush and rode down into the river bed.

There might have been a dozen, or even twenty, and although I could not make them out I could see white streaks on their faces that meant they were painted for war.

Crossing the stream sixty, seventy yards below me they rode out across the prairie. They would not be moving this late unless there was a camp not far off, and that meant more Indians and a possible source of trouble.

When they had gone I went back to camp and got Cap Rountree. Together, we talked to Torres and made what plans we could.

Daylight came, and on the advice of Torres, Drusilla remained with the wagons. We moved slowly, trying to keep our dust down.

It was dry . . . the grass was brown, parched and sun-hot when we fetched up to Owl Creek and found it bone-dry. Little and Big Cow Creeks, also dry.

This last was twenty miles from our last night's camp and no sign of water, with another twenty to go before we reached the Bend of the Arkansas.

"There'll be water," Rountree said in his rasping voice, "there's always water in the Arkansas."

By that time I wasn't sure if there was any water left in Kansas. We took a breather at Big Cow Creek and I rinsed out Dapple's mouth with my handkerchief a couple of times. My lips were cracked and even Dapple seemed to have lost his bounce. That heat and the dry air, with no water, it was enough to take the spry out of a camel.

Dust lifted from the brown grass . . . white buffalo bones bleached in the sun. We passed the wrecks of some burned-out wagons and the skull of a horse. In the distance clouds piled up enormous towers and battlements, building dream castles in the sky. Along the prairie, heat waves danced and rippled in the sun, and far off a mirage lake showed the blue of its dream water to taunt our eyes.

From the top of a low hill I looked around at miles of brown emptiness with a vast sweep of sky overhead where the sun seemed to have grown enormously until it swept the sky. From my canteen I soaked my handkerchief and sponged out the Dapple's mouth, again. It was so dry I couldn't spit.

Far below the wagons made a thin trail . . . the hill on which I sat was low, but there was a four-mile-long slope leading gradually up to it.

The horizon was nowhere, for there was only a haze of heat around us, our horses slogging onward without hope, going because their riders knew no better.

The sky was empty, the land was still . . . the dust hung in the empty air. It was very hot.

Chapter IV

ROUNTREE HUMPED his old shoulders under his thin shirt and looked ready to fall any minute but the chances were he would outlast us all. There was iron and rawhide in that old man.

Glancing back I saw a distant plume of dust, and pointed it out to Orrin who gave an arm signal to Torres. We got down from our horses, Orrin and I, and walked along to spell our mounts.

"We got to get that place for Ma," I said to Orrin, "she ain't got many years. Be nice if she could live them in comfort, in her own home, with her own fixin's."

"We'll find it."

Dust puffed from each step. Pausing to look back, he squinted his eyes against the glare and the sting of sweat. "We got to learn something, Tye," he said suddenly, "we're both ignorant, and it ain't a way to be. Listening to Tom makes a man think. If a body had an education like that, no telling how far he'd go."

"Tom's got the right idea. In this western land a man could make something of himself."

"The country makes a man think of it. It's a big country with lots of room to spread out . . . it gives a man big ideas."

When we got back into the saddle the leather was so hot on my bottom I durned near yelled when I settled down into my seat.

After awhile, country like that, you just keep moving putting one foot ahead of the other like a man in a trance. It was dark with the stars out when we smelled green trees, grass, and the cool sweetness of water running. We came up to the Arkansas by starlight and I'd still a cup of brackish water in my canteen. Right away, never knowing what will happen, I dumped it out, rinsed the canteen and filled it up again.

Taking that canteen to Drusilla's wagon I noticed Baca watching me with a hard look in his eyes. She was too good for either of us.

The four of us built our own fire away from the others because we had business to talk.

"The don has quite a place, Torres tells me. Big grant of land. Mountains, meadows, forest . . . and lots of cattle." Cap had been talking to Torres for some time. "Runs sheep, too. And a couple of mines, a sawmill."

"I hear he's a land hog," Orrin commented. "Lots of folks would like to build homes there, if he'd let 'em."

"Would you, Orrin, if you owned the land?" Tom asked mildly.

"Nobody has a right to all that. Anyway, he ain't an American," Orrin insisted.

Rountree was no hand to argue but he was a just old man. "He's owned that land forty years, and he got it from his father who moved into that country back in 1794. Seems they should have an idea of who it belongs to."

"Maybe I was mistaken," Orrin replied. "That was what I'd heard."

"Don Luis is no pilgrim," Rountree told us, "I heard about him when I first come west. He and his pappy, they fought Utes, Navajo, and Comanches. They worked that land, brought sheep and cattle clear from Mexico, and they opened the mines, built the sawmill. I reckon anybody wants to take their land is goin' to have to dig in an' scratch."

"It doesn't seem to me that Jonathan Pritts would do anything that isn't right," Orrin argued. "Not if he knows the facts."

Pawnee Rock was next . . . Torres came over to our fire to tell us Don Luis had decided to fight shy of it.

Orrin wanted to see it and so did I, so the four of us decided to ride that way while the wagons cut wide around it.

Forty or fifty men were camped near the Rock, a tough, noisy, drunken crowd, well supplied with whiskey.

"Looks like a war party," Rountree commented.

Suddenly I had a bad feeling that this was the Pritts crowd, for I could think of no reason why a bunch of that size should be camping here without wagons or women. And I saw one of them who had been with the Back Rand crowd the other side of Abilene.

When they saw us riding up, several got up from where they'd been loafing. "Howdy! Where you from?"

"Passing through." Tom Sunday glanced past the few men who had come to greet us at their camp, which was no decent camp, but dirty, untidy and casual. "We're headed for the upper Cimarron," he added.

"Why don't you step down? We got a proposition for you."

"We're behind time," Orrin told him, and he was looking at their faces as if he wanted to remember them.

Several others had strolled toward us, sort of circling casually around as if they wanted to get behind us, so I let the dapple turn to face them.

They didn't take to that, not a little bit, and one redhead among them took it up. "What's the matter? You afraid of something?"

When a man faces up to trouble with an outfit like that you get nowhere either talking or running, so I started the dapple toward him, not saying a word, but walking the horse right at him. My right hand was on my thigh within inches of my six-shooter, and it sized up to me like they figured to see what would happen if Red crowded me.

Red started to side-step but the dapple was a cutting horse Pa had used working stock, and once you pointed that horse at anything, man or animal, he knew what his job was.

Red backed off, and long ago I'd learned that when you get a man to backing up its hard for him to stop and start coming at you. Every move he made the dapple shifted and went for him, and all of a sudden Red got desperate and grabbed for his gun and just as he grabbed I spurred the dapple into him. The dapple hit him with a shoulder and Red went down hard. He lost grip on the pistol which fell several feet away.

Red lay on the ground on his back with the dapple right over him, and I hadn't said a word.

While everybody was watching the show Red and the dapple were putting on, Orrin had his pistol lying there in his lap. Both Tom Sunday and Cap Rountree had their rifles ready and Cap spoke up. "Like I said, we're just passing through."

Red started to get up and the dapple shifted his weight and Red relaxed. "You get up when we're gone, Red. You're in too much of a sweat to get killed."

Several of the others had seen what was going on and started toward us.

"All right, Tye?" Orrin asked.

"Let's go," I said, and we dusted out of there.

One thing Cap had in mind and I knew it was what he was thinking. If they were watching us they wouldn't have noticed the passing of the wagons, and they didn't. We watered at Coon Creek and headed for Fort Dodge.

The Barlow, Sanderson Company stage came in while we were in Fort Dodge. Seems a mighty fine way to travel, sitting back against the cushions with nice folks around you.

We were standing there watching when we heard the stage driver talking to a sergeant. "Looks like a fight shaping up over squatters trying to move in on the Spanish grants," he said.

Orrin turned away. "Good thing we're staying shut of that fight," he said. "We'll be better off hunting cows."

When we rode back to camp everything was a-bustle with packing and loading up.

Torres came to us. "We go, señores. There is word of trouble from home. We take the dry route south from here. You will not come with us?"

"We're going to the Purgatoire."

"Then it will be adios." Torres glanced at me. "I know that Don Luis will wish to say good-by to you, señor."

At the wagons Don Luis was nowhere in sight, but Drusilla was. When she saw me she came quickly forward. "Oh, Tye! We're going! Will I ever see you again?"

"I'll be coming to Santa Fe. Shall I call on you then?"

"Please do."

We stood together in the darkness with all the hurry around us of people packing and getting ready to move, the jingle of trace chains, the movement and the shouts.

Only I felt like something was going right out from my insides, and I'd never felt this way before. Right then I didn't want to hunt wild cows. I wanted to go to Santa Fe. Was this the way Orrin felt about Laura Pritts?

But how could I feel any way at all about her? I was a mountain boy who could scarcely read printing and who could not write more than his name.

"Will you write to me, Tyrel?"

How could I tell her I didn't know how? "I'll write," I said, and swore to myself that I'd learn. I'd get Tom to teach me.

Orrin was right. We would have to get an education, some way, somehow.

"I'll miss you."

Me, like a damned fool I stood there twisting my hat. If I'd only had some of Orrin's easy talk! But I'd never talked much to any girl or even womenfolks, and I'd no idea what a man said to them.

"It was mighty fine," I told her, "riding out on the plains with you."

She moved closer to me and I wanted to kiss her the worst way, but what right had a Tennessee boy to kiss the daughter of a Spanish don?

"I'll miss the riding," I said, grasping at something to say. "I'll sure miss it."

She stood on her tiptoes suddenly and kissed me, and then she ran. I turned right around and walked right into a tree. I backed off and started again and just then Antonio Baca came out of the darkness and he had a knife held low down in his hand. He didn't say anything, just lunged at me.

Talking to girls was one thing, cutting scrapes was something else. Pa had brought me up right one way, at least. It was without thinking, what I did. My left palm slapped his knife wrist over to my right to get the blade out of line with my body, and my right hand dropped on his wrist as my left leg came across in front of him, and then I just spilled him over my leg and threw him hard against a tree trunk.

He was in the air when he hit it, and the knife fell free. Scooping it up, I just walked on and never even looked back. One time there, I figured I heard him groan, but I was sure he was alive all right. Just shook up.

Tom Sunday was in the saddle with my dapple beside him. "Orrin and Cap went on. They'll meet us at the Fort."

"All right," I said.

"I figured you'd want to say good-by. Mighty hard to leave a girl as pretty as that."

30

I looked at him. "First girl ever paid me any mind," I said. "Girls don't cotton to me much."

"As long as girls like that one like you, you've nothing to worry about," he said quietly. "She's a real lady. You've a right to be proud."

Then he saw the knife in my hand. Everybody knew that knife who had been with the wagons. Baca was always flashing it around.

"Collecting souveniers?" Tom asked dryly.

"Wasn't planning on it." I shoved the knife down in my belt. "Sort of fell into it."

We rode on a few steps and he said, "Did you kill him?"

"No."

"You should have," he said, "because you'll have it to do."

Seems I never had a difficulty with a man that made so little impression. All I could think of was Drusilla Alvarado, and the fact that we were riding away from her. All the time I kept telling myself I was a fool, that she was not for me. But it didn't make a mite of difference, and from that day on I understood Orrin a lot better and felt sorry for him.

Nothing changed my mind about that narrow-between-the-ears blonde, though. That roan horse never had been any account, and miserable, contrary and ornery it was, too.

We could see the lights of the Fort up ahead and behind me the rumble of those wagon wheels as the train moved out, the rattle of trace chains, and the Mexicans calling to each other.

"Tom," I said, "I got to learn to write. I really got to learn."

"You should learn," he told me seriously, "I'll be glad to teach you."

"And to read writing?"

"All right."

We rode in silence for a little while and then Tom Sunday said, "Tye, this is a big country out here and it takes big men to live in it, but it gives every man an equal opportunity. You're just as big or small as your vision is, and if you've a mind to work and make something of yourself, you can do it."

He was telling me that I could be important enough for even a don's daughter, I knew that. He was telling me that and suddenly I did not need to be told. He was right, of course, and all the time I'd known it. This was a country to grow up in, a land where a man had a chance.

The stars were bright. The camp lay far behind. Somebody in the settlement ahead laughed and somebody else dropped a bucket and it rolled down some steps.

A faint breeze stirred, cool and pleasant. We were making the first step. We were going after wild cows.

We were bound for the Purgatoire.

Chapter V

CAP ROUNTREE had trapped beaver all over the country we were riding toward. He had been there with Kit Carson, Uncle Dick Wootton, Jim Bridger, and the Bents. He knew the country like an Indian would know it.

Tom Sunday . . . I often wondered about Tom. He was a Texan, he said, and that was good enough. He knew more about cattle than any of us.

Orrin and me, well, most of what we'd had all our lives came from our own planting or hunting, and we grew up with a knowledge of the herbs a man can eat and how to get along in the forest.

The country we were riding toward was Indian country. It was a place where the Comanches, Utes, Arapahos, and Kiowas raided and fought, and there were Cheyennes about, too. And sometimes the Apaches raiding north. In this country the price for a few lazy minutes might be the death of every man in the party. It was no place for a loafer or one lacking responsibility.

Always and forever we were conscious of the sky. City folks almost never look at the sky to the stars but with us there was no choice. They were always with us.

Tom Sunday was a man who knew a sight of poetry, and riding across the country thataway, he'd recite it for us. It was a lonely life, you know, and I expect what Sunday missed most was the reading. Books were rare and treasured things, hard to come by and often fought over. Newspapers the same.

A man couldn't walk down to the corner and buy a paper. Nor did he have a postman to deliver it to him. I've known cowhands to memorize the labels off canned fruit and vege-tables for lack of reading.

Cap knew that country, knew every creek and every fork. There were no maps except what a man had in his skull, and nobody of whom to ask directions, so a body remem-bered what he saw. Cap knew a thousand miles of country like a man might know his kitchen, to home.

These mornings the air was fresher. There was a faint chill in the air, a sign we were getting higher. We were riding along in the early hours when we saw the wagons.

Seven wagons, burned and charred. We moved in carefully, rifles up and ready; edged over to them, holding to a shallow dip in the prairie until we were close up.

Folks back east have a sight to say about the poor Indian but they never fought him. He was a fighter by trade, and because he naturally loved it, mercy never entered his head.

Mercy is a taught thing. Nobody comes by it natural. Indians grew up thinking the tribe was all there was and anybody else was an enemy.

It wasn't a fault, simply that nobody had ever suggested such a thing to him. An enemy was to be killed, and then cut up so if you met him in the afterlife he wouldn't have the use of his limbs to attack you again. Some Indians believed a mutilated man would never get into the hereafter.

Two of the men in this outfit had been spread-eagled on wagon wheels, shot full of arrows, and scalped. The women lay scattered about, their clothing ripped off, blood all over. One man had got into a buffalo wallow with his woman and had made a stand there.

"No marks on them," I said, "they must have died after the Indians left."

"No," Cap indicated the tracks of moccasins near the bodies. "They killed themselves when their ammunition gave out." He showed us powder burns on the woman's dress and the man's temple. "Killed her and then himself."

The man who made the stand there in the wallow had accounted for some Indians. We found spots of blood on the grass that gave reason to believe he'd killed four or five, but Indians always carry their dead away.

"They aren't mutilated because the man fought well. Indians respect a fighter and they respect almost nobody else. But sometimes they cut them up, too."

We buried the two where they lay in the wallow, and the others we buried in a common grave nearby, using a shovel found near one of the wagons.

Cap found several letters that hadn't burned and put them in his pocket. "Least we can do," he said, "the folks back home will want to know."

Sunday was standing off sizing up those wagons and looking puzzled. "Cap," he said, "come over here a minute."

The wagons had been set afire but some had burned hardly at all before the fire went out. They were charred all over, and the canvas tops were burned, of course.

33

"See what you mean," Orrin said, "seems to be a mighty thick bottom on that wagon."

"Too thick," Sunday said, "I think there's a false bottom."

Using the shovel he pried a board until we could get enough grip to pull it loose. There was a compartment there, and in it a flat iron box, which we broke open.

Inside were several sacks of gold money and a little silver, coming to more than a thousand dollars. There were also a few letters in that box.

"This is better than hunting cows," Sunday said. "We've got us a nice piece of money here."

"Maybe somebody needs that money," Orrin suggested. "We'd better read those letters and see if we can find the owner."

Tom Sunday looked at him, smiling but something in his smile made a body think he didn't feel like smiling. "You aren't serious? The owner's dead."

"Ma would need that money mighty bad if it had been sent to her by Tyrel and me," Orrin said, "and it could be somebody needs this money right bad."

First off, I'd thought he was joking, but he was dead serious, and the way he looked at it made me back up and take another look myself. The thing to do was to find who the money rightfully belonged to and send it to them . . . if we found nobody then it would be all right to keep it.

Cap Rountree just stood there stoking that old pipe and studying Orrin with care, like he seen something mighty interesting.

There wasn't five dollars amongst us now. We'd had to buy pack animals and our outfit, and we had broke ourselves, what with Orrin and me sending a little money to Ma from Abilene. Now we were about to start four or five months of hard work, and risk our hair into the bargain, for no more money than this.

"These people are dead, Orrin," Tom Sunday said irritably, "and if we hadn't found it years might pass before anybody else did, and by that time any letter would have fallen to pieces."

Standing there watching the two of them I'd no idea what was happening to us, and that the feelings from that dispute would affect all our lives, and for many years. At the time it seemed such a little thing.

"Not in this life will any of us ever find a thousand dollars in gold. Not again. And you suggest we try to find the owner."

"Whatever we do we'd better decide somewheres else," I commented. "There might be Indians around."

Come dusk we camped in some trees near the Arkansas, bringing all the stock in close and watering them well. Nobody did any talking. This was no place to have trouble but when it came to that, Orrin was my brother . . . and he was in the right.

Now personally, I'm not sure I'd have thought of it. Mayhap I wouldn't have mentioned it if I did think of it . . . a man never knows about things like that. Rountree hadn't done anything but listen and smoke that old pipe of his.

It was when we were sitting over coffee that Tom brought it up again. "We'd be fools not to keep that money, Orrin. How do we know who we'd be sending it to? Maybe some relative who hated him. Certainly, nobody needs it more than we do."

Orrin, he just sat there studying those letters. "Those folks had a daughter back home," Orrin said, finally, "an' she's barely sixteen. She's living with friends until they send for her, and when those friends find out she isn't going to be sent for, and they can expect no more money, then what happens to that girl?"

The question bothered Tom, and it made him mad. His face got red and set in stubborn lines, and he said, "You send your share. I'll take a quarter of it . . . right now. If I hadn't noticed that wagon the money would never have been found."

"You're right about that, Tom," Orrin said reasonably, "but the money just ain't ours."

Slowly, Tom Sunday got to his feet. He was mad clear through and pushing for a fight. So I got up, too.

"Kid," he said angrily, "you stay out of this. This is between Orrin and me."

"We're all in this together, Cap an' me as much as Orrin and you. We started out to round up wild cattle, and if we start it with trouble there's no way we can win."

Orrin said, "Now if that money belonged to a man, maybe I'd never have thought of returning it, but with a girl as young as that, no telling what she'll come to, turned loose on the world at that age. This money could make a lot of difference."

Tom was a prideful and stubborn man, ready to take on the two of us. Then Rountree settled matters.

"Tom," he said mildly, "you're wrong, an' what's more, you know it. This here outfit is four-sided and I vote with the Sackett boys. You ain't agin democracy, are you, Tom?"

"You know darned well I'm not, and as long as you put it that way, I'll sit down. Only I think we're damned fools."

"Tom, you're probably right, but that's the kind of a

damned fool I am," said Orrin. "When the cows are rounded up if you don't feel different about it you can have my share of the cows."

Tom Sunday just looked at Orrin. "You damned fool. Next thing we know you'll be singing hymns in a church."

"I know a couple," Orrin said. "You all set down and while Tyrel gets supper, I'll sing you a couple."

And that was the end of it . . . or we thought it was. Sometimes I wonder if anything is ever ended. The words a man speaks today live on in his thoughts or the memories of others, and the shot fired, the blow struck, the thing done today is like a stone tossed into a pool and the ripples keep widening out until they touch lives far from ours.

So Orrin sang his hymans, and followed them with *Black, Black, Black, Lord Randall, Barbara Allan* and *Sweet Betsy*. When Orrin finished the last one Tom reached over and held out his hand and Orrin grinned at him and shook it.

No more was said about the gold money and it was put away in the bottom of a pack and to all intents it was forgotten. If that amount of gold is ever forgotten.

We were getting into the country of the wild cattle now. Cap Rountree as well as others had noticed these wild cattle, some of them escaped from Spanish settlements to the south, and some escaped or stampeded by Indians from wagon trains bound for California.

No doubt Indians had killed a few, but Indians preferred buffalo, and many of these cattle had come south with buffalo herds. There was no shortage of buffalo in 1867, and the Indians only killed the wild cattle when there was nothing else.

The country we were going to work lay south of the Mountain Branch of the Santa Fe Trail, between the Purgatoire and Two Buttes Creek, and south to the Mal Pais. It was big country and it was rough country. We rode south through sage plains with some mesquite, with juniper and piñon on the hills.

Cap had in his mind a hidden place, a canyon near the base of a mountain where a cold spring of sweet water came out of the rocks. There was maybe two hundred acres of good grass in the bottom, grass belly-high to a horse, and from the look of it nobody had seen it since Cap Rountree stumbled on it twenty years back.

First off, we forted up. Behind us the cliffs lifted sheer with an overhang that provided shelter from above. Right out in front there was four or five acres of meadow with good grass, edged on the far side by trees and rocks. Beyond that was the bowl with the big pasture as we called it, and in an adjoining canyon was a still larger area where we figured to trap the wild cattle and hold them.

We spent that first day gathering fuel, adding a few rocks to our fort, and generally scouting the country close around our hide-out. Also, I killed a deer and Cap got a buffalo. We brought the meat into camp and started jerking it.

Next morning at daybreak we started out to scout the country. Within an hour's riding we'd seen sixty or seventy head. A man never saw such cattle. There was a longhorn bull in that crowd that must have stood seven feet and would have weighed sixteen hundred pounds. And horns? Needle-sharp.

By nightfall we had a good bunch of cattle in the bowl or drifted toward it. By the third day we had more than a hundred head in that bowl and we were beginning to count our money.

It was slow, patient work. Push them too fast and they would stampede clear out of the country, so we tried to move them without them guessing what we planned.

We had two things to accomplish: to catch ourselves some wild cattle and to stay alive while doing it. And it wasn't only Indians we had to think about, but the cattle themselves, for some of those tough old bulls showed fight, and the cows could be just as mean if they caught a man afoot. Of a night we yarned around the fire or belly-ached about somebody's cooking. We took turn about on that job.

We kept our fires small, used the driest wood, and we moved around only when we had to. We daren't set any patterns of work so's Indians could lay for us. We never took the same trail back that we used on the way out, and we kept our eyes open all the time.

We gathered cattle. We sweated, we swore, and we ate dust, but we gathered them up, six one day, twelve another, nineteen, then only three. There was no telling how it would be. We got them into the bowl where there was grass and plenty of water and we watched them get fat. Also, it gave them time to settle down.

Then trouble hit us. Orrin was riding a sorrel we had picked up in Dodge. He was off by himself and he started down a steep hillside and the sorrel fell. That little sorrel got up fast with Orrin's foot caught in the stirrup and he buckled down to run. There was only one way Orrin could keep from being dragged to death, and that was one reason cowhands always carried pistols. He shot the sorrel.

Come nightfall there was no sign of Orrin. We had taken to coming in early so if anything went wrong with any of us there would be time to do something before night.

37

We set out to look. Tom went south, swinging back toward the east, Cap went west, and I followed up a canyon to the north before topping out on the rim. It was me found him, walking along, packing his saddle and his Winchester.

When he put down the saddle on seeing me, I rode up to him. "You took long enough," he grumbled, but there was no grumble in his eyes, "I was fixing to cache my saddle."

"You could have fired a shot."

"There were Indians closer than you," he said.

Orrin told us about it around the fire. He had shucked his saddle off the dead sorrel and started for camp, but being a sly one, he was not about to leave a direct trail to our hide-out, so he went downhill first and stumbled on a rocky ledge which he followed sixty or seventy yards.

There had been nine or ten Indians in the party and he saw them before they saw him, so he just laid right down where he was and let them pass by. They were all warriors, and the way they were riding they might miss his dead horse.

"They'll find it," Cap told us, "it's nigh to dark now, so they won't get far tonight. Likely they'll camp somewhere down the creek. At daybreak they'll see the buzzards."

"So?"

"That's a shod horse. It isn't likely they'd pass up a chance to get one man afoot and alone."

Any other time we could have high-tailed it out of the country and left them nothing but tracks, but now we were men of property and property ties a man down.

"Think they'll find us?"

"Likely," Cap said. "Reckon we better hold to camp a day or two. Horses need the rest, anyway."

We all sat there feeling mighty glum, knowing the chances were that if the Indians didn't find us they would stay around the country, looking for us. That meant that our chance of rounding up more cattle was coming down to nothing.

"You know what I think?" They waited for me to speak up. "I think we should cash in our chips. I think we should take what we've got and hit the trail for Santa Fe, sell what we've got, and get us a proper outfit. We need three or four horses per man for this kind of work."

Tom Sunday flipped his bowie knife into the sand, retrieved it and studied the light on the blade while he gave it thought. "Not a bad idea," he said.

"Cap?"

"If Orrin's willin'." Cap hesitated. "I figure we should dust out of here, come daybreak."

"Wasn't what I had in mind," I said, "I meant to leave
38

right now . . . before those Indians find that sorrel."

The reason I hadn't waited for Orrin to speak was because I knew he was pining to see that yellow-haired girl and I had some visiting in mind my own self.

Only it wasn't that . . . it was the plain, common-sense notion that once those Indians knew we were here, starting a herd might be tough to do. It might take them a day or two to work out our trail. Chances were by the time they found we were gone we'd be miles down the trail.

So I just picked up my saddle and headed for my horse. There is a time that calls for action and when debate makes no sense. Starting a herd in the middle of the night isn't the best thing to do, but handling cattle we'd be scattered out and easy picking for Indians, and I wanted to get started.

We just packed up and lit out. Those cattle were heavy with water and grass and not in the mood for travel but we started them anyhow. We put the north star at our backs and started for Santa Fe.

When the first sun broke the gray sky we had six miles behind us.

Chapter VI

WE HAD our troubles. When that bunch began to realize what was happening they didn't like it. We wore our horses to a frazzle but we kept that herd on the trail right up to dusk to tire them out as much as to get distance behind us. We kept a sharp lookout, but we saw no Indians.

Santa Fe was a smaller town than we expected, and it sure didn't shape up to more than a huddle of adobe houses built around a sunbaked plaza, but it was the most town I'd ever seen, or Orrin.

Folks stood in the doorways and shaded their eyes at us as we bunched our cows, and then three riders, Spanish men, started up the trail toward us. They were cantering their horses and staring at us, then they broke into a gallop and came charging up with shrill yells that almost started our herd again. It was Miguel, Pete Romero, and a rider named Abreu.

"Ho!" Miguel was smiling. "It is good to see you, *amigo*. We have been watching for you. Don Luis has asked that you be his guests for dinner."

"Does he know we're here?" Orrin was surprised.

Miguel glanced at him. "Don Luis knows most things, *señor*. A rider brought news from the Vegas."

They remained with the herd while we rode into town. We walked over to the La Fonda and left our horses in the shade. It was cool inside, and quiet. It was shadowed there like a cathedral, only this here was no cathedral. It was a drinking place, and a hotel, too, I guess.

Mostly they were Spanish men sitting around, talking it soft in that soft-sounding tongue of theirs, and it gave me a wonderful feeling of being a travelled man, of being in foreign parts. A couple of them spoke to us, most polite.

We sat down and dug deep for the little we had. Wasn't much, but enough for a few glasses of wine and mayhap something to eat. I liked hearing the soft murmur of voices, the clink of glasses, and the click of heels on the floor. Somewhere out back a woman laughed, and it was a mighty fine sound.

While we sat there an Army officer came in. Tall man, thirtyish with a clean uniform and a stiff way of walking like those Army men have. He had mighty fancy mustaches.

"Are you the men who own those cattle on the edge of town?"

"Are you in the market?" Orrin said.

"That depends on the price."

He sat down with us and ordered a glass of wine.

"I will be frank, gentlemen, there has been a drought here and a lot of cattle have been lost. Most of the stock is very thin. Yours is the first fat beef we've seen."

Tom Sunday glanced up and smiled. "We will want twenty-five dollars per head."

The captain merely glanced at him. "Of course not," he said, then he smiled at us and lifted his glass. "Your health—"

"What about Don Luis Alvarado?" Orrin asked suddenly.

The captain's expression stiffened a little and he asked, "Are you one of the Pritts crowd?"

"No," Tom Sunday said, "we met the don out on the Plains. Came west from Abilene with him, as a matter of fact."

"He's one of those who welcomed us in New Mexico. Before we took over the Territory the Mexican government was in no position to send troops to protect these colonies from the Indians. Also, most of the trade was between Santa Fe and the States, rather than between Santa Fe and Mexico. The don appreciated this, and most of the people here welcomed us."

"Jonathan Pritts is bringing in settlers," Orrin said.

"Mr. Pritts is a forceful and energetic man," the captain said, "but he is under the false impression that because New Mexico has become a possession of the United States . . . I should say, a part of the United States . . . that the property rights of all Spanish-speaking people will be tossed out the window."

There was a pause. "The settlers—if one wishes to call them that—that Jonathan Pritts is bringing in are all men who bring their guns instead of families."

I had me another glass of wine and sat back and listened to the captain talking with Tom Sunday. Seems the captain was out of that Army school, West Point, but he was a man who had read a sight of books. A man never realizes how little he knows until he listens to folks like that talk. Up where I was born we had the Bible, and once in awhile somebody would bring a newspaper but it was a rare thing when we saw any other kind of reading.

Politics was a high card up in the hills. A political speech would bring out the whole country. Folks would pack their picnic lunches and you'd see people at a speech you'd never see elsewhere. Back in those days 'most every boy grew up knowing as much about local politics as about coon dogs, which was about equal as to interest.

Orrin and me, we just set and listened. A man can learn a lot if he listens, and if I didn't learn anything else I was learning how much I didn't know. It made me hungry to know it all, and mad because I was getting so late a start.

We'd picked up a few more head of cattle coming south and the way it was going to figure out, each of us would have more than a thousand dollars of his own when we'd settled up. Next day Orrin and Cap went to the stage office and arranged to ship east the gold we'd found in the wagon.

The itch to see the town got the best of me so I walked outside. Those black-eyed *señoritas* was enough to turn a man's good sense. If Orrin would look at some of these girls he'd forget all about Laura. It was no wonder he fell for her. After a man has been surrounded for months by a lot of hard-handed, hairy-chested men even the doggiest kind of female looks mighty good.

Most of all right now I wanted a bath and a shave. Cap, he followed me.

"Seems to me there's things around town need seeing to," I suggested.

"You look here, Tyrel, if you're thinkin' of what I think you're thinkin' you'd better scout the country and study the sign before you make your move. If you figure to court a Spanish gal you'd also better figure to fight her man."

41

"Seems like it might be worth it."

This was siesta time. A dog opened one eye and wagged a tail to show that if I didn't bother him he'd be pleased. Me, I wasn't of a mind to bother anybody.

Taking it slow, I walked down the dusty street. The town was quiet. A wide door opened into a long, barnlike building with a lot of tubs and water running through in a ditch. There was homemade soap there and nobody around. There was a pump there, too. It was the first time I ever saw a pump inside a house. Folks are sure getting lazy . . . won't even go outside the house to pump.

This here must be a public bathhouse, but there was nobody around to take my money. I filled a tub with water, stripped off and got in and when I'd covered with soap, head to foot, three women came in with bundles of clothes on their heads.

First off I stared and they stared and then I yelled. All of a sudden I realized this here was no bathhouse but a place to wash clothes.

Those Spanish girls had taken one look and then they began to shriek, and first off I figured they were scared, but they weren't running, they were just standing there laughing at me.

Laughing!

Grabbing a bucket of water I doused myself with it and grabbed up a towel. Then they ran outside and I could hear screams and I never crawled into my clothes so fast in all my born days. Slinging gun belt around me at a dead run I beat it for my horse.

It must have been a sight, me all soapy in that tub. Red around the gills. I started Dapple out of town on a run and the last thing I could hear was laughter. Women sure do beat all.

Anyway, I'd had a bath.

Morning was bright and beautiful like nine mornings out of ten in the high desert country. We met the captain and turned the cattle over to him. We'd finally settled on twenty dollars a head, which was a very good price at the time and place.

First off, as we rode into town, a girl spotted me. She pointed her finger at me, gasped, and spoke excitedly to the girl with her, and then they both began to look at me and laugh.

Orrin was puzzled because the girls always noticed him first and paid me no mind. "Do you know those girls?"

"Me? I never saw them before in my life." But it gave me

a tip-off as to what it was going to be like. That story must be all over Santa Fe by now.

Before we reached the La Fonda we'd passed a dozen girls and they all laughed or smiled at me. Tom Sunday and Orrin, they hadn't an idea of what was going on.

The La Fonda was cool and pleasant again, so we ordered wine and a meal. The girl who took our order realized all of a sudden who I was and she began to giggle. When she went out with our order, two or three girls came from the kitchen to look at me.

Picking up a glass of wine, I tried to appear worldly and mighty smug about it all. Fact was, I felt pretty foolish.

Orrin was getting sore. He couldn't understand this sudden interest the girls were taking in me. He was curious, interested and kind of jealous all to once. Only thing I could do was stand my ground and wear it out or high-tail it for the brush.

Santa Fe was a small town, but it was a friendly town. Folks here all wanted the good time that strangers brought. Those years, it was a town at the end of things, although it was old enough to have been a center of everything. And the girls loved a fandango and enjoyed the presence of the Americans.

There was a cute little button of a Mexican girl and every time I'd see her she'd give me a flashing glance out of those big dark eyes, and believe me, I'd get flustered.

This one had a shape to take a man's eye. Every time she'd pass me on the streets she'd give a little more swish to her skirts and I figured we could get acquainted if I just knew how to go about it. Her name was Tina Fernandez.

Night of the second day, there was a knock at the door and when I opened it Fetterson was standing there.

"Mr. Pritts wants to see you, all of you. He wants to talk business."

We looked at each other, then Orrin got up to go. The rest of us followed him and a Mexican standing at the bar turned his back on us. Anybody who was friendly to Jonathan Pritts would find few friends in Santa Fe.

It wasn't just that which worried me. It was Orrin.

Jonathan Pritts had four men outside the adobe where he lived and a few others loafing near the corral. Through the bunkhouse door I could see several men, all armed.

One thing you've got to watch, Tyrel, I told myself, is a man with so many fighters around. He wouldn't have all those men unless he figured he'd need them.

Rountree glanced at me. He was badger tough and coon smart. Sunday paused on the porch and took out a cigar; when he reached back and struck the match on his pants three chairs creaked as men put their hands to their guns. Tom didn't let on he noticed but there was a sly smile around his mouth.

Laura came to meet us in a blue dress that brought out the blue in her eyes, so she looked like an angel. The way she offered both hands to Orrin and the way she looked at him . . . it was enough to make a man gag. Only Orrin wasn't gagging. He was looking like somebody had hit him with a fence post.

Cap was uncommon sour but Sunday—always a hand with the ladies—gave her a wide smile. Sometimes I thought it irritated him that Laura had chosen to fall for Orrin and not him.

Her eyes looked past Orrin at me and our minds were hitched to the same idea. We simply did not like each other.

Jonathan Pritts entered wearing a preacher's coat and a collar that made you wonder whether he was going to offer prayer or sell you a gold brick.

He passed around a box of cigars and I was glad I didn't smoke. Orrin accepted a cigar, and after the slightest hesitation, Tom did too.

"I don't smoke," I said.

"Will you have a drink?"

"I don't drink," I said.

Orrin looked at me, because while I don't care for the stuff I sometimes drink with friends.

"You boys have done well with your cattle," Pritts said, "and I like men with business minds. However, I am wondering what you plan to do with the proceeds of your success. I can use men who want to invest business brains and capital, men who can start something and carry it through."

Nobody said anything and he brushed the ash from his cigar and studied the glowing end for a minute.

"There may be a little trouble at first. The people on the land are not Americans and may resent our moving in."

Orrin spoke slowly. "Tyrel and me came west hunting land. We're looking for a home."

"Good! New Mexico is now a part of the United States, and it's time that we American citizens had the benfits."

He drew deep on his cigar. "The first comers will be first served."

"The way it sounds," I said, "you plan to shove out the first comers and move in yourself."

Pritts was mad. He was not accustomed to straight talk—

least of all from men like us. He said nothing for a moment and Laura sat down near Orrin and I got a whiff of her perfume.

"The Mexicans have no rights," Pritts replied. "The land belongs to us freeborn Americans, and if you come in with us now you will have shares in the company we are forming."

"We need a home for Ma," Orrin said, "we do need land."

"If we get it this way, there'll be blood on it," I said, "but first we should get Mr. Pritts' proposition in writing, just what he has in mind, and how he aims to settle up." That was Pa talking. Pa always said, "Get it in writing, boy."

"A gentleman's word," Pritts replied stiffly, "should be enough."

I got up. I'd no idea what the others figured to do and didn't much care. This sanctimonious old goat was figuring to steal land from folks who'd lived on it for years.

"A man who is talking of stealing land with guns," I said, "is in no position to talk about himself as being a gentleman. Those people are American citizens now as much as you or me."

Turning around, I started for the door, and Cap Rountree was only a step behind me. Tom Sunday hesitated, being a polite man, but the four of us were four who worked and travelled together, so he followed us. Orrin lagged a little, but he came.

Pritts yelled after us, his voice trembling he was so mad. "Remember this! Those who aren't with me are against me! Ride out of town and don't come back!"

None of us were greenhorns and we knew those men on the porch weren't knitting so when we stopped, the four of us faced out in four directions. "Mr. Pritts," I said, "you've got mighty big ideas for such a small head. Don't you make trouble for us or we'll run you back to the country they run you out of."

He was coming after us and he stopped in midstride, stopped as though I'd hit him with my fist. Right then I knew what I'd said was true . . . somebody had run him out of somewhere.

He was an arrogant man who fancied himself important, and mostly he carried it off, but now he was mad. "We'll see about that!" he shouted. "Wilson, *take them!*"

Rountree was facing the first man who started to get out of a chair, which was Wilson, and there was no mercy in old Cap. He just laid a gun barrel alongside of Wilson's head and Wilson folded right back into his chair.

The man facing Orrin had a six-shooter in his stomach and I was looking across a gun barrel at Pritts himself.

"Mr. Pritts," I said, "you're a man who wants to move in on folks with guns. Now you just tell them to go ahead with what they've started and you'll be dead on the floor by the time you've said it."

Laura stared at me with such hatred as I've ever seen on a woman's face. There was a girl with a mighty big picture of her pa and anybody who didn't see her pa the way she did couldn't be anything but evil. And whoever she married was always going to play second fiddle to Jonathan Pritts.

Pritts looked like he'd swallowed something that wasn't good for him. He looked at that Navy Colt and he knew I was not fooling. And so did I.

"All right." He almost choked on it. "You can go."

We walked to our horses with nobody talking and when we were in our saddles Orrin turned on me. "Damn you, Tye, you played hell. You the same as called him a thief."

"That land belongs to Alvarado. We killed a lot of Higginses for less."

That night I slept mighty little, trying to figure out if I'd done right. Anyway I looked at it, I thought I'd done the right thing, and I didn't believe my liking for Drusilla had a thing to do with it. And believe me, I thought about that.

Next morning I saw Fetterson riding out of town with a pack of about forty men, and Wilson was with him. Only Wilson's hat wasn't setting right because of the lump on his skull. They rode out of town, headed northeast.

About the time they cleared the last house a Mexican boy mounted on a speedy looking sorrel took off for the hills, riding like the devil was on his tail.

Looked to me like Don Luis had his own warning system and would be ready for Fetterson before he got there. Riding that fast he wouldn't be riding far, so chances were a relay of horses was waiting to carry the word. Don Luis had a lot of men, lots of horses, and a good many friends.

Orrin came out, stuffing his shirt into his pants. He looked mean as a bear with a sore tooth. "You had no call to jump Mr. Pritts like that."

"If he was an honest man, I'd have nothing to say."

Orrin sat down. One thing a body could say for Orrin, he was a fair man. "Tyrel," he said at last, "you ought to think before you talk. I like that girl."

Well . . . I felt mighty mean and low down. I set store by Orrin. Most ways he was smarter than me, but about this Pritts affair, I figured he was wrong.

"Orrin, I'm sorry. We never had much, you and me. But what we had, we had honest. We want a home for Ma. But it wouldn't be the home she wants if it was bought with blood."

"Well . . . damn it, Tyrel, you're right, of course. I just wish you hadn't been so rough on Mr. Pritts."

"I'm sorry. It was me, not you. You ain't accountable for the brother you've got."

"Tyrel, don't you talk thataway. Without you that day back home in Tennessee I'd be buried and nobody knows it better than me."

Chapter VII

THIS WAS raw, open country, rugged country, and it bred a different kind of man. The cattle that went wild in Texas became the longhorn, and ran mostly to horns and legs because the country needed a big animal that could fight and one who could walk three days to get water. Just so it bred the kind of man with guts and toughness no eastern man could use.

Most men never discover what they've got inside. A man has to face up to trouble before he knows. The kind of conniving a man could get away with back east wouldn't go out here. Not in those early years. You can hide that sort of behavior in a crowd, but not in a country where there's so few people. Not that we didn't have our own kinds of trickery and cheating.

Jonathan Pritts was one of those who mistook liberty for license and he figured he could get away with anything. Worst of all, he had an exaggerated idea of how big a man he was . . . trouble was, he wasn't a big man, just a mean one.

We banked our money with the Express Company in Santa Fe, and then we saddled up and started back to the Purgatoire after more cattle. We had us an outfit this time. Dapple was still my horse, and a better no man was likely to have, but each of us now had four extra mounts and I'd felt I'd done myself proud.

The first was a *grulla*, a mouse-colored mustang who, judging by disposition, was sired out of a Missouri mule by a mountain lion with a sore tooth. That *grulla* was the most irritating, cantankerous bit of horseflesh I ever saw, and he could buck like a sidewinder on a red-ant hill. On the other hand he could go all day and night over any kind of country on less grass and water than one of Beale's camels. My name for him was Sate, short for Satan.

There was a buckskin, a desert horse used to rough going, but steady. In many ways the most reliable horse I had. His name was Buck, like you might expect.

Kelly was a big red horse with lots of bottom. Each horse I paid for out of my own money, although Sate they almost gave me, glad to be rid of him, I expect.

First time I straddled Sate we had us a mite of a go-around. When I came off him I was shook up inside and had a nosebleed, but I got off when I was good and ready and from that time on Sate knew who was wearing the pants.

My fourth horse I bought from an Indian.

We'd spent most of the day dickering with Spanish men, and this Indian sat off to one side, watching. He was a big-framed Nez Perce from up Idaho, Montana way.

He was at the corral at sunup and by noontime I'd not seen him have a bite to eat.

"You're a long way from home," I said, slicing off a chunk of beef I'd had fixed for a lunch and handed it to him.

He looked at me, a long, careful look, then he accepted it. He ate slow like a starving man who can't eat a lot at first because his stomach shrinks up.

"You speak English?"

"I speak."

Splitting my grub down the middle, I gave him half, and we ate together. When we'd finished he got up. "Come—you see horse."

The horse was a handsome animal, a roan with a splash of white with red spots on the white, the kind of horse they call an appaloosa. Gaunt as his owner he stood a good sixteen hands. Looked like this Indian had come a long way on short rations.

So I swapped him my old rifle (I'd bought a .44 Henry the day before) and some grub. I threw in my old blanket.

We were a week out of Santa Fe when we found a spot in the bend of a creek among some rocks. When we'd forted up they left it to me to scare up some fresh meat as we planned to live off the country and stretch our store-bought rations.

That Montana horse could move. He could get out and go, lickety-brindle, and he was smart. We passed up antelope because no matter what folks tell you it's the worst kind of Rocky Mountain meat. Old-timers will tell you that cougar meat is best. Lewis and Clark said that, and Jim Bridger,

Kit Carson, Uncle Dick Wootton, Jim Baker . . . they all agreed.

Morning, with a bright sun over far hills, shadows lying in the folds and creases of the country, sunlight on cottonwood leaves and sparkling on the river water . . . a meadow lark calling. Montana horse and me, we sure loved it. We took off along an old deer trail. This was higher country than before, the plateaus giving way to long ridges crested with pines and slopes dotted with juniper or piñon.

Suddenlike, I saw a deer . . . and then another. Tethering Montana horse I moved up with my rifle.

Feeding deer are easy to stalk if a man is careful on his feet and doesn't let them get wind of him. When deer put their heads down to graze, you can move up on them, and you can keep moving, very quiet. When their tails start to switch they're going to look up, so you freeze in position. He may be looking right at you when he looks up, and he might look a long time, but if you stand right still, after awhile he will decide you're a harmless tree or stump and go back to feeding.

I worked my way up to within fifty yards of a good big buck and then I lifted my rifle and put a bullet behind the left foreleg. There was another deer no further off and on my left, and as I fired at the first one I swung the rifle just as he was taking his first jump and my bullet broke his neck as he hit ground.

Working fast, I butchered those deer, loaded the choice cuts into their hides and mounted Montana horse. When I came out of the trees a couple of miles further on a half-dozen buffalo were running across the wind. Now no buffalo runs without reason.

Pulling up on the edge of the trees I knew we'd be hard to see, for that roan and me with my buckskin outfit fitted into the country like part of it. No man in this country ever skylines himself if he can help it.

Sometimes the first man to move is the first to die, so I waited. The sun was bright on the hillside. My horse stamped a foot and switched his tail. A bee hummed around some leaves on a bush nearby.

They came in a single file, nine of them in a row. Utes, from the description I'd heard from Cap. They came out of the trees and angled along the slope in front of me.

Now most times I prefer to stand my ground and fight it out for running can make your back a broad target, but there are times to fight and times to run and the wise man is one who can choose the right time for each.

First off, I sat still, but they were riding closer and closer to me, and if they didn't see me their horses would. If I tried to go back into the trees they'd hear me.

Sliding my rifle across my saddle I said a prayer to the guardian angel of fools and covered maybe thirty yards before they saw me. One of them must have spoken because they all looked.

Indians can make mistakes like anybody. If they had all turned and come at me I'd have had to break for the brush and I'd have been fairly caught. But one Indian got too anxious and threw up his rifle and fired.

Seeing that rifle come up, I hit the spurs to Montana horse and went away from there, but in the split seconds before I hit him with the spurs, I fired. As I'd been timing my horse's steps I'd shot at the right time and I didn't miss.

My shot took out, not the Indian shooting at me but the one who seemed to be riding the best horse. My shot was a hair ahead of his and he missed when Montana horse jumped.

We took out . . . and I mean we really lit a shuck. There was nothing around there I wanted and what I wanted most was distance from where I was.

With that first Indian down I'd cut my sign right across their trail and now they wanted me mighty bad, but that horse didn't like Utes any better than I did. He put his ears back and stretched out his tail and left there like a scared rabbit.

My next shot was a miss. With Montana horse travelling like he'd forgot something in Santa Fe, there wasn't much chance of a hit. They had all come right at me with the shooting and I saw unless I did something drastic they had me so I swung and charged right at the nearest Indian. He was fifty yards ahead of the nearest Ute and which shot got his horse I don't know, but I fired three or four shots at him.

Dust jumped from the horse's side and the horse went down throwing his rider over his head into the grass, and when I went by at a dead run I shot into that Indian as I rode.

They were all messed up for a minute or two, switching directions and running into each other, but meanwhile I rode through a small creek and was out on the open prairie beyond.

We were eight to ten miles from camp and I wasn't about to lead these Utes full tilt into my friends. And then I saw a buffalo wallow.

Slowing Montana horse we slid into that wallow and I hit ground and threw my shoulder into the horse and grabbed his off foreleg, hoping to throw him, but Montana horse seemed to know just what I wanted and he went down and rolled on his side like he had been trained for it . . . which he probably had, the Nez Perce using appaloosas for war horses.

Dropping to one knee, the other leg stretched out ahead of me, I drew a careful bead on the chest of the nearest Ute and squeezed off my shot.

There was a minute when I believed I'd missed, and him coming right into my sights, then his horse swung wide and dumped a dead Ute into the grass. There was a bright stain of blood on the horse's side as he swung away.

It was warm and still. Patting Montana horse I told him, "You rest yourself, boy, we'll make out."

He rolled his eyes at me like he understood every word.

You would never have believed that a moment ago there was shooting and killing going on, because suddenly everything was still. The hillside was empty, those Indians had gone into the ground faster than you would believe. Lying there, knowing any moment might be my last, I liked the feel of the warm sun on my back, the smell of parched brown grass and of dust.

Three of the Utes were down in the grass and there were six left. Six to one might seem long odds but if a man has nerve enough and if he thinks in terms of combat, the advantage is often against sheer numbers. Sheer numbers rob a man of something and he begins to depend . . . and in a fighting matter no man should depend. He should do what has to be done himself.

My canteen was full and I'd some jerked meat in my saddlebag, lots of fresh meat, and plenty of ammunition.

They would try to come over the rise behind me. That crest, only a couple of feet away, masked my view of the far slope. So I had out my bowie knife and began cutting a trench. That was a nine-inch blade, sharp enough to shave with, and I worked faster than ever in my born days.

It took me only minutes to have a trench that gave me a view of the back slope, and I looked around just in time. Four of them were coming up the slope toward me on foot and running bent over. My shot was a miss . . . too quick. But they hit dirt. Where there had been running Indians there was only grass stirring in the wind.

They would be creeping on their bellies now, getting closer. Taking a chance, I leaped up. Instantly, I spotted a crawling Indian and fired, then dropped into my hole with bullets spearing the air where I'd been. That was something I couldn't try again, for now they'd be expecting.

Overhead there were high streamers of white clouds. Turning around I crawled into my trench, and just in time. An Indian was coming up that back slope, bent over and coming fast and I let him come. It was high time I shortened the odds against me, so I put my rifle in position, reached down to ease my Colt for fast work in case the others closed in at the same time. That Ute was going to reach me with his next rush.

Some were down, but I doubted if more than one was actually dead. I wasn't counting any scalps until I had them.

Minutes loitered. Sweat trickled down my cheeks and my neck. I could smell the sweat of my own body and the hot dust. Somewhere an eagle cried. Sweat and dust made my skin itch, and when a big horsefly lit on Montana, my slap sounded loud in the hot stillness.

Eastern folks might call this adventure, but it is one thing to read of adventure sitting in an easy chair with a cool drink at hand, and quite another thing to be belly down in the hot dust with four, five Indians coming up the slope at you with killing on their minds.

A grasshopper flew into the grass maybe fifteen yards down slope, then took off at once, quick and sharp. That was warning enough. Lifting the rifle I steadied it on that spot for a quick shot, then chanced a glance over my shoulder. Just as I looked back that Ute charged out of the grass like he was bee-stung.

My guess had been right, and he came up where that grasshopper had lit. My sights were on the middle of his chest when I squeezed off my shot and he fell in plain sight.

Behind me their feet made a whisper in the dry grass and rolling over I palmed my Colt and had two shots off before I felt the slam of the bullet. The Utes vanished and then I was alone but for a creeping numbness in my left shoulder and the slow welling of blood.

Sliding back from the trench I felt sickish faint and plugged the hole with a handkerchief. The bullet had gone through and I was already soaked with blood on my left side. With bits of handkerchief I plugged the bullet hole on both sides and knew I was in real trouble.

Blinking against the heat and sudden dizziness I fed shells into my guns. Then I took the plug from my canteen and rinsed my mouth. It was lukewarm and brackish.

My head started to throb heavily and it was an effort to move my eyebrows. The smell of sweat and dried grass grew stronger and overhead the sky was yellow and hot as brass. From out of an immeasurable distance a buzzard came.

Suddenly I hated the smells, hated the heat, hated the

buzzard circling and patient—as it could be patient—knowing that most things die.

Crawling to the rim of the buffalo wallow my eyes searched the terrain before me, dancing with heat waves. I tried to swallow and could not, and Tennessee and its cool hills seemed very far away.

Through something like delirium I saw my mother rocking in her old chair, and Orrin coming up from the spring with a wooden bucket full of the coldest water a man could find.

Lying in a dusty hole on a hot Colorado hillside with a bullet hole in me and Utes waiting to finish the job, I suddenly remembered what day it was.

It had been an hour . . . or had it been more? It had been at least an hour since the last attack. Like the buzzards, all those Utes needed was time, and what is time to an Indian?

Today was my birthday . . . today I was nineteen years old.

Chapter VIII

LONG FINGERS of shadow reached out from the sentinel pines before I took my next swallow of water. Twice I'd sponged out the mouth of that Montana horse, who was growing restless and harder to keep down.

No chance to take a cat nap, or even take my eyes off the country for more than a minute because I knew they were still out there and they probably knew I was hurt. My shoulder was giving me billy-hell. Even if I'd had a chance to run for it Montana horse would be stiff from lying so long.

About that time I saw the outfit coming up the slope. They rode right up to that buffalo wallow bold as brass and sat their horses grinning at me, and I was never so glad to see anybody.

"You're just in time for tea," I said, "you all just pull up your chairs. I've got the water on and she'll be ready any minute."

"He's delirious," Tom Sunday grinned like a big ape. "He's gone off his rocker."

"It's the heat," Orrin agreed. "The way he's dug in you'd think he'd been fighting Indians."

"Hallucinations," Rountree added, "a plain case of prairie sickness."

"If one of you will get off his horse," I suggested, "I'll plain whip him till his hair falls out, one-handed at that. Where've you been? Yarning it in the shade?"

"He asks us where we've been?" Sunday exclaimed. "And him sitting in a nice cool hole in the ground while we work our fool heads off."

Rountree, he cut out and scouted around, and when he rode back he said, "Looks like you had yourself a party. By the blood on the grass you got two, anyway."

"You should backtrack me." I was feeling ornery as a stepped-on baby. "If I didn't score on five out of nine Utes, I'll put up money for the drinks."

"Only three took off when we showed up," Sunday agreed.

Grabbing my saddle horn I pulled myself into the leather; for the first time since I'd sighted those Utes I could count on another day of living.

For the next three days I was cook which comes of having a bum wing on a cow outfit. Cap was a fair hand at patching up wounds and he made a poultice of herbs of some kind which he packed on my shoulder. He cleaned the wound by running an arrow shaft through with a cloth soaked in whiskey, and if you think that's entertainment, you just try it on for size.

On the fifth day I was back in the saddle but I fought shy of Sate, reckoning he'd be too much for me, feeling like I was. So I worked Dapple and Buck to a frazzle, and ended up riding Montana horse who was turning into a real cow horse.

This was rougher country than before. We combed the breaks and drifted the cattle into a rough corral. It was hot, rough, cussing work, believe you me. Here and there we found some branded stock, stuff that had stampeded from trail herds further east, or been driven off by Indians.

"Maybe we should try Abilene this time," I suggested to the others. "The price would be better. We just happened to be lucky in Santa Fe."

Seven hundred head of cattle was what we started out with, and seven hundred head can be handled by four men if they work like dogs and are passing lucky.

As before, we let them graze as they moved. What we wanted was fat cattle at selling time. In that box canyon they had steadied down a good bit with plenty of water and grass and nothing much to do but eat and lie around.

First night out from the Purgatoire we bedded down after

a long drive with the cattle mighty tired. After awhile Orrin stopped near me.

"Tyrel, I sure wish you and Laura cottoned to each other more'n you do."

"If you like her, Orrin, that's what matters. I can't be no different than I am, and something about her doesn't ring true. Orrin, the way I see it, you'd always play second fiddle to her old man."

"That's not true," He said, but there wasn't much force in it.

After awhile we met again and stopped together. "Ma's not getting younger," he said, "and we've been gone a year."

A coyote made talk to the stars, but nothing else seemed to be stirring.

"If we sell this herd we'll have more money than any Sackett ever heard of, and I figure we should buy ourselves an outfit and start ranching. Then we ought to get some book learning. Especially you, Orrin. You could make a name for yourself."

Orrin's thoughts were afar off for a minute or two, gathering dreams somewhere along tomorrow's road.

"I've had it in mind," he said finally.

"You've a talking way with you, Orrin. You could be governor."

"I haven't the book learning."

"Davy Crockett went to Congress. Andrew Johnson was taught to read and write by his wife. I figure we can get the book learning. Hell, man, if youngsters can learn we should be able to throw it and hog-tie it. I figure you should study law. You've got a winning way with that Welsh tongue of yours."

We drove through Dodge on to Abilene, and that town had spread itself all over the prairie, with saloons side by each, all of them going twenty-four hours to the day, and packed most of the time.

Everywhere a man looked around the town there were herds of Texas cattle. "We came to the wrong market," Cap said dourly, "we should have sold out in Dodge."

We swung the herd into a tight circle and saw several riders coming toward us. Two of them looked like buyers and the other two looked like trouble. Orrin did his talking to the first two, Charlie English and Rosie Rosenbaum. Rosenbaum was a stocky man with mild blue eyes, and I could tell by the way he was sizing up our cattle that he knew beef.

"How many head have you got?" he asked Orrin.

"Seven hundred and forty, as of last night," Orrin said, "and we want a fast deal."

The other two had been studying our herd and sizing us up.

"I should think you would," one of them said, "those are stolen cattle."

Orrin just looked at him. "My name is Orrin Sackett, and I never stole anything in my life." He paused. "And I never had anything stolen from me, either."

The man's face shadowed. "You've got Two-Bar cattle in that herd," he said, "and I'm Ernie Webb, foreman of the Two-Bar."

"There are Two-Bar cows in that herd, and we rounded them up in the Colorado country along with a lot of wild cattle. If you want to claim them get your boss and we'll talk a deal, but he'll pay for the rounding up and driving."

"I don't need the boss," Webb replied, "I handle my own trouble."

"Now see here," Rosenbaum interfered quietly. "There's no need for this. Sackett is reasonable enough. Get your boss and when the matter is settled, I'll buy."

"You stay out of this." Webb was staring at Orrin, a trouble-hunting look on his face. "This is a rustled herd and we're taking it over."

Several rough-looking riders had been drifting closer, very casually. I knew a box play when I saw one.

Where I was sitting Webb and his partner couldn't see me because Sunday was between us. They'd never seen Orrin before but they'd both seen me that day on the plains of east Kansas.

"Cap," I said, "if they want it, let's let them have it."

"Tom," I wheeled my horse around Sunday which allowed me to flank Webb and his partner, "this man may have been foreman for Two-Bar once, but he also rode with Back Rand."

Cap had stepped down from his saddle and had his horse between himself on the oncoming riders, his rifle across his saddle. "You boys can buy the herd," Cap said, "but you'll buy it the hard way."

The riders drew up.

Rosenbaum was waiting right in the middle of where a lot of lead could be flying but there wasn't a quiver in him. For a man with no stake in the deal, he had nerve.

Webb had turned to look at me, and Orrin went on like he hadn't been interrupted. "Mr. Rosenbaum, you buy these cattle and keep track of any odd brands you find. I think they'll check with those in our tally books, and we'll post

56

bond for their value and settle with any legitimate claimant but nobody is taking any cattle from us."

Ernie Webb had it all laid out for him nice and pretty, and it was his turn to call the tune. If he wanted to sashay around a bit he had picked himself four men who could step to the music.

"It's that loudmouth kid," Webb said, "somebody will beat it out of him someday, and then rub his nose in it."

"You try," Orrin invited. "You can have any one of us, but that kid will blow you loose from your saddle."

We sold out for thirty-two dollars a head, and Rosenbaum admitted it was some of the fattest stock brought into Abilene that year. Our herd had grazed over country no other herds travelled and with plenty of water. We'd made our second lucky drive and each of us had a notion we'd played out our luck.

When we got our cash we slicked out in black broadcloth suits, white shirts, and new hats. We were more than satisfied and didn't figure to do any better than what we had.

Big John Ryan showed up to talk cattle. "This the Sackett outfit?"

"We're it."

"Hear you had Tumblin' R stock in your herd?"

"Yes, sir. Sit down, will you?" Orrin told him about it. "Seven head, including a brindle steer with a busted horn."

"That old devil still alive? Nigh cost me the herd a few times and if I'd caught him I'd have shot him. Stampede at the drop of a hat and take a herd with him."

"You've got money coming, Mr. Ryan. At thirty-two dollars a head we figure—"

"Forget it. Hell . . . anybody with gumption enough to round up those cows and drive them over here from Colorado is entitled to them. Besides, I just sold two herds of nearly six thousand head . . . seven head aren't going to break me."

He ordered a drink. "Fact is, I'd like to talk to you boys about handling my herd across the Bozeman Trail."

Orrin looked at me. "Tom Sunday is the best cattleman among us. Orrin and me, we want to find a place of our own."

"I can't argue with that. My drive will start on the Neuces and drive to the Musselshell in Montana. How about it, Sunday?"

"I think not. I'll trail along with the boys."

There I sat with almost six thousand dollars belonging to me and about a thousand more back in Sante Fe, and I was scared. It was the first time in my life I'd ever had anything to lose.

The way I saw it unless a man knows where he's going he isn't going anywhere at all. We wanted a home for Ma, and a ranch, and we also wanted enough education to face the changing times. It was time to do some serious thinking.

A voice interrupted. "Aren't you Tyrel Sackett?"

It was the manager of the Drovers' Cottage. "There's a letter for you."

"A letter?" I looked at him stupidly. Nobody had ever written me a letter.

Maybe Ma . . . I was scared. Who would write to me?

It looked like a woman's handwriting. I carefully unfolded the letter. It scared me all hollow.

Worst of it was, the words were handwritten and the letters were all which-way and I had a time making them out. But I wet my lips, dug in my heels, and went to work—figuring a man who could drive cattle could read a letter if he put his mind to it.

First off there was the town: Santa Fe. And the date. It was written only a week or so after we left Santa Fe.

Dear Mr. Sackett:

Well, now! Who was calling me mister? Mostly they called me Tyrel, or Tye, or Sackett.

The letter was signed *Drusilla.*

Right about then I started to get hot around the neck and ears, and took a quick look to see if anybody noticed. You never saw so many people paying less attention to anybody.

They heard I was in Santa Fe and wondered why I did not visit them. There had been trouble when some men had tried to take part of the ranch but the men had gone away. All but four, which they buried. And then her grandfather had gone to town to see Jonathan Pritts. In my mind's eyes I could see those two old men facing each other, and it must have been something to see, but my money was on the don. She ended with an invitation to visit them when I was next in Santa Fe.

Time has a way of running out from under a man. Looked like a man would never amount to much without book learning and every day folks were talking of what they read, of what was happening, but none of it made sense to me who had to learn by listening. When a man learns by listening he is never sure whether he is getting the straight of things or not.

There was a newspaper that belonged to nobody and I took that; it took me three days to work my way through its four pages.

There was a man in town with gear to sell, and figuring on buying an extra pistol, I went to see him. The gun I bought, and some boxes of shells, but when I saw some books in his wagon I bought them without looking.

"You don't want to know what they are?"

"Mister, I don't see that's your business, but the fact is, I wouldn't know one from the other. I figured if I studied out those books I'd learn. I'd work it out."

He had the look of a man who knew about writing and printing. "These aren't the books I'd recommend for a beginner, but you may get something out of them."

He sold me six books and I took them away.

Night after night I sat by the campfire plugging away at those books, and Tom Sunday sure helped a lot in telling me what words were about. First off, I got a surprise by learning that a man could learn something about his own way of living from a book. This book by an Army man, Captain Randolph Marcy, was written for a guide to parties traveling west by wagon. He told a lot of things I knew, and a good many I didn't.

Cap Rountree made out like he was sour about the books. "Need an extry pack horse for all that printed truck. First time I ever heard of a man packin' books on the trail."

Chapter IX

SANTA FE lay lazy in the sun when we rode into town. Nothing seemed to have changed, yet there was a feeling of change in me. And Drusilla was here, and this time I would call at her home. I'd never called on a girl before.

My letter from Drusilla was my own secret and I had no idea of telling anyone about it. Not even Orrin.

When Drusilla wrote I didn't answer because I couldn't write and if I'd traced the letters out—well, it didn't seem right that a man should be writing like a child.

First off when we got to Santa Fe I wanted to see Drusilla, so I went about getting my broadcloth suit brushed and pressed out. It was late afternoon when I rode to the ranch. Miguel was loafing at the gate with a rifle across his knees.

"*Señor*! It is good to see you! Every day the *señorita* has asked me if I have seen you!"

"Is she in?"

"*Señor*, it is good that you are back. Good for them, and good for us too." He indicated the door.

The house surrounded a patio, and stood itself within an adobe wall fifteen feet high. There was a walk ran around the inside near the top of the wall, and there were firing positions for at least thirty men on that wall.

Don Luis sat working at a desk. He arose. "Good afternoon, señor. It is good to see you. Was your venture a success?"

So I sat down and told him of our trip. A few of the cattle had carried his brand and we had kept the money for him and this I now paid.

"There is much trouble here," Don Luis said. "I fear it is only the beginning."

It seemed to me he had aged a lot in the short time since I'd last seen him. Suddenly, I realized how much I liked that stern, stiff old man with his white mustache.

Sitting back in his chair, he told me how Pritts' men made their first move. Forty in the group had moved on some flat land well within the Grant and had staked claims there, then they had dug in for a fight. Knowing the manner of men he faced, Don Luis held back his *vaqueros*.

"There are, *señor,* many ways to victory, and not all of them through violence. And if there was a pitched battle, some of my men would be hurt. This I wished to avoid."

The invaders were watched, and it was noted when Pritts and Fetterson returned to Santa Fe on business that several bottles appeared and by midnight half the camp was drunk. Don Luis was close by, but he held back his *vaqueros* who were eager for a fight.

By three in the morning when all were in a drunken sleep, Don Luis' *vaqueros* moved in swiftly.

The invaders were tied to their horses and started back down the road toward Santa Fe. Their tents and equipment were burned or confiscated, their weapons unloaded and returned to them. They were well down the trail when several riders returning from Mora engaged in a running gun battle with the *vaqueros*. Four of the invaders were killed, several wounded. Don Luis had two men wounded, none seriously.

"The advantage was ours," Don Luis explained, "but Jonathan Pritts is a very shrewd man and he is making friends, nor is he a man to suffer defeat without retaliation. It is difficult," he added, "to carry out a project with the sort of men he uses. They are toughs and evil men."

"Don Luis," I said, "have I your permission to see Miss Drusilla?"

He arose. "Of course, señor. I fear if the privilege were

denied that I should have another war, and one which I am much less suited to handle.

"We in New Mexico," he added, "have been closer to your people than our own. It is far to Mexico City, so our trade has been with you, our customs affected by yours. My family would disapprove of our ways, but on the frontier there is small time for formality."

Standing in the living room of the lovely old Spanish home, I felt stiff in my new clothes. Abilene had given me time to get used to them, but the awkwardness returned now that I was to see Drusilla again.

I could hear the click of her heels on the stone flags, and turned to face the door, my heart pounding, my mouth suddenly so dry I could scarcely swallow.

She paused in the doorway, looking at me. She was taller than I had remembered, and her eyes were larger. She was beautiful, too beautiful for a man like me.

"I thought you had forgotten us," she said, "you didn't answer my letter."

I shifted my hat in my hands. "It looked like I'd get here as fast as the letter, and I'm not much hand at writing."

An Indian woman came in with some coffee and some little cakes and we both sat down. Drusilla sat very erect in her chair, her hands in her lap, and I decided she was almost as embarrassed as I was.

"Ma'am, I never called on a girl before. I guess I'm almighty awkward."

Suddenly, she giggled. "And I never received a young man before," she said.

After that we didn't have much trouble. We both relaxed and I told her about our trip, about rounding up wild cattle and my fight with the Indians.

"You must be very brave."

Well, now. I liked her thinking that about me but fact is, I hadn't thought of much out there but keeping my head and tail down so's not to get shot, and I recalled being in something of a sweat to get out of there.

I've nothing against a man being scared as long as he does what has to be done . . . being scared can keep a man from getting killed and often makes a better fighter of him.

We sat there in that cool, spacious room with its dark, massive furniture and tiled floors and I can tell you it was a wonderful friendly feeling. I'd never known a house like that before, and it seemed very grand and very rich.

Dru was worried about her grandfather. "He's getting

61

old, Tyrel, and I'm afraid for him. He doesn't sleep well, and sometimes he paces the floor all night long."

Torres was waiting for me when I went to get my horse almost an hour later. "Señor," he said carefully, "Don Luis likes you and so does the señorita. Our people, they like you too."

He studied me searchingly. "Señor Pritts hates us, and he is winning friends among your people. He spends much money. I believe he would take everything from us."

"Not while I'm alive."

"We need a sheriff in this country, a man who will see justice done." He looked at me. "We ask only for justice."

"What you say is true. We do need a sheriff."

"The don grows old, and he does not know what to do, but all my life I have been with him, señor, and I do not think that to fight is enough. We must do something else, as your people would. There are, señor, still more Mexicans than Anglos. Perhaps if there was an election. . . ."

"A Mexican sheriff would not be good, Juan. The Americans would not be willing to recognize him. Not those who follow Pritts."

"This I know, señor. We will talk of this again."

When I walked into the La Fonda that night Ollie Shaddock was standing at the bar having a drink. He was a broad man with a shock of blond hair and a broad, cheerful face.

"Have a drink," he said, "I resigned my sheriffing job to bring your Ma and the boys west."

"You brought Ma?"

"Sure enough. Orrin's with her now."

He filled my glass from the bottle. "Don't you be thinkin' of me as sheriff. You done right in killin' Long. I'd have had to arrest you but the law would have freed you. He had a gun pointed when you killed him."

We didn't say anything more about it. It was good to have Ollie Shaddock out here, and I owed him a debt for bringing Ma. I wanted to see her the worst way but Ollie had something on his mind.

"Folks talk you up pretty high," he said.

"It's Orrin they like."

"You know something, Tyrel? I've been giving some thought to Orrin since I got here. He's a man should run for office."

It seemed a lot of folks had running for office on their minds, but this was a new country and in need of law. "He's got it in mind," I said.

"I've been in politics all my years. I was a deputy sheriff

at seventeen, sheriff at nineteen, justice of the peace at twenty-four and served a term in the state legislature before I was thirty. Then I was sheriff again."

"I know it."

"Orrin looks to me like a man who could get out the vote. Folks take to him. He talks well, and with a mite more reading he could make something of himself, if we managed it right."

"We?"

"Politics ain't much different, Tyrel, than one of these icebergs you hear tell of. Most of what goes on is beneath the surface. It doesn't make any difference how good a man is, or how good his ideas are, or even how honest he is unless he can put across a program, and that's politics.

"Statesmanship is about ten percent good ideas and motives and ninety percent getting backing for your program. Now I figure I know how to get a man elected, and Orrin's our man. Also, you can be a big advantage to him."

"Folks don't take to me."

"Now that's as may be. I find most of the Mexicans like you. They all know you and Orrin turned Pritts down when he invited you to join him, and the *vaqueros* from the Alvarado ranch have been talking real friendly about you."

He chuckled. "Seems the women like you too. They tell me you provided more entertainment in one afternoon than they had in years."

"Now, look—!" I could feel myself getting red around the ears.

"Don't let it bother you. Folks enjoyed it, and they like you. Don't ask me why."

"You seem to have learned a lot since you've been here."

"Every man to his job, mine's politics. First thing is to listen. Learn the issues, the personalities, where the votes are, where the hard feelings are."

Ollie Shaddock tasted his whiskey and put the glass back on the bar. "Tyrel, there's trouble brewing and it will come from that Pritts outfit. That's a rough bunch of boys and they'll get to drinking and there'll be a killing. Chances are, it will be a riot or something like that."

"So?"

"So we got to go up there. You and me and Orrin. When that trouble comes Orrin has to handle it."

"He's no officer."

"Leave that to me. When it happens, folks will want somebody to take over the responsibility. So Orrin steps in."

He tossed off his whiskey. "Look . . . Pritts wants Torres killed, some of the other key men. When the shooting starts

63

some of those fur thieves and rustlers he's got will go too far.

"Orrin steps in. He's Anglo, so all the better Americans will be for him. You convince the Mexicans Orrin is their man. Then we get Orrin appointed marshal, run him for sheriff, start planning for the legislature."

Ollie made a lot of sense, and it beat all how quickly he had got hold of the situation, and him here only a few weeks. Orrin was the man for it all right. Or Tom Sunday.

"What about Tom Sunday?"

"He figures he's the man for the job. But Tom Sunday can't talk to folks like Orrin can. He can't get down and be friends with everybody the way Orrin can. Orrin just plain likes people and they feel it . . . like you like Mexicans and they know it. Anyway," he added, "Orrin is one of ours and one thing about Orrin. We don't have to lie."

"Would you lie?"

Ollie was embarrassed. "Tyrel, politics is politics, and in politics a man wants to win. So he hedges a little."

"Whatever we do has to be honest," I said. "Look, I'm no pilgrim. But there's nothing in this world I can't get without lying or cheating. Ma raised us boys that way, and I'm glad of it."

"All right, honesty is a good policy and if a man's honest it gets around. What do you think about Orrin?"

"I think he's the right man."

Only as I left there and started to see Ma, I was thinking about Tom Sunday. Tom was our friend, and Tom wasn't going to like this. He was a mite jealous of Orrin. Tom had the best education but folks just paid more mind to Orrin.

Ma had aged . . . she was setting in her old rocker which Ollie had brought west in his wagon, and she had that old shawl over her knees. When I walked in she was puffing on that old pipe and she looked me up and down mighty sharp.

"You've filled out. Your Pa would be proud of you."

So we sat there and talked about the mountains back home and of folks we knew and I told her some of our plans. Thinking how hard her years had been, I wanted to do something for her and the boys. Bob was seventeen, Joe fifteen.

Ma wasn't used to much, but she liked flowers around her and trees. She liked meadow grass blowing in the wind and the soft fall of rain on her own roof. A good fire, her rocker, a home of her own, and her boys not too far away.

Ollie Shaddock wasted no time but rode off toward Mora. He was planning on buying a place, a saloon, or some such place where folks could get together. In those days a saloon was a meeting place, and usually the only one.

Of the books I'd bought I'd read Marcy's guide books first, and then that story, *The Deerslayer*. That was a sure enough good story too. Then I read Washington Irving's book about traveling on the prairies, and now was reading Gregg on *Commerce of the Prairies*.

Reading those books was making me talk better and look around more and see what Irving had seen, or Gregg. It was mighty interesting.

Orrin and me headed for the hills to scout a place for a home. Sate was feeling his oats and gave me a lively go-around but I figured the trip would take some of the salt out of him. That Satan horse really did like to hump his back and duck his head between his legs.

We rode along, talking land, cattle, and politics, and enjoying the day. This was a far cry from those blue-green Tennessee mountains, but the air was so clear you could hardly believe it, and I'd never seen a more beautiful land. The mountains were close above us, sharp and clear against the sky, and mostly covered with pines.

Sate wasn't cutting up any more. He was stepping right out like he wanted to go somewhere, but pretty soon I began to get a feeling I didn't like very much.

Sometimes a man's senses will pick up sounds or glimpses not strong enough to make an impression on him but they affect his thinking anyway. Maybe that's all there is to instinct or the awareness a man develops when he's in dangerous country. One thing I do know, his senses become tuned to sounds above and below the usual ranges of hearing.

We caught, of a sudden, a faint smell of dust on the air. There was no wind, but there was dust.

We walked our horses forward and I watched Sate's ears. Those ears pricked up, like the mustang he was, and I knew he was aware of something himself.

My eyes caught an impression and I walked my horse over for a look where part of the bark was peeled back from a branch. There were horses' tracks on the ground around the bush.

"Three or four, wouldn't you say, Tyrel?"

"Five. This one is different. The horses must have stood here around two hours, and then the fifth one came up but he didn't stop or get down."

Several cigarette butts were under a tree near where the horses had been tethered, and the stub of a black cigar.

We were already further north than we had planned to

go and suddenly it came to me. "Orrin, we're on the Alvarado grant."

He looked around, studied our back trail and said. "I think it's Torres. Somebody is laying for him."

He walked his horse along, studying tracks. One of the horses had small feet, a light, almost prancing step. We both knew that track. A man who can read sign can read a track the way a banker would a signature. That small hoof and light step, and that sidling way of moving was Reed Carney's show horse.

Whoever the others had been, and the chances were Reed Carney had joined up with Fetterson and Pritts, they had waited there until the fifth man came along to get them. And that meant he could have been a lookout, watching for the man they were to kill.

Now we were assuming a good deal. Maybe. But there was just nothing to bring a party up here . . . not in those days.

Orrin shucked his Winchester.

It was pine timber now and the trail angled up the slope through the trees. When we stopped again we were high up and the air was so clear you could see for miles. The rim was not far ahead.

We saw them.

Four riders, and below on the slope a fifth one, scouting. And off across the valley floor, a plume of dust that looked like it must be the one who was to be the target.

The men were below us, taking up position to cover a place not sixty yards from their rifles. They were a hundred feet or so higher than the rider, and he would be in the open.

Orrin and me left our horses in the trees. We stood on the edge of the mesa with a straight drop of about seventy feet right ahead of us, then the talus sloped away steeply to where the five men had gathered after leaving their horses tied to the brush a good hundred yards off.

They were well concealed from below. There was no escape for them, however, except to right or left. They could not come up the hill, and they could not go over the rim.

Orrin found himself a nice spot behind a wedged-up slab of rock. Me, I was sizing up a big boulder and getting an idea. That boulder sat right on the edge of the mesa, in fact it was a part of the edge that was ready to fall . . . with a little help.

Now I like to roll rocks. Sure, it's crazy, but I like to see them roll and bounce and take a lot of debris with them. So I walked to the rim, braced myself against the trunk of a gnarled old cedar and put my feet against the edge of that rock.

The rider they were waiting for was almost in sight. When I put my boots against that rock my knees had to be doubled up, so I began to push. I began to straighten them out. The rock crunched heavily, teetered slightly, and then with a slow, majestic movement it turned over and fell.

The huge boulder hit with a heavy thud and turned over, gained speed, and rolled down the hill. The riders glanced around and seemed unable to move, and then as that boulder turned over and started to fall, they scattered like sheep.

At the same instant, Orrin lifted his rifle and put a bullet into the brush ahead of their horses. One of the broncs reared up and as Orrin fired again, he jerked his head and ripping off a branch of the brush, broke free and started to run, holding his head to one side to keep from tripping on the branch.

The lone horseman had come into sight, and when he stared up the mountain, I lifted my hat and waved, knowing from his fawn-colored sombrero that it was Torres. Doubtfully, he lifted a hand, unable to make us out at that distance.

One of the men started for their horses and Orrin put a bullet into the ground ahead of him and the man dove for shelter. Orrin levered another shot into the rocks where he disappeared then sat back and lighted up one of those Spanish cigars.

It was downright hot. Settling in behind some rocks I took a pull at my canteen and figured down where they were it had to be hotter than up here where we had some shade.

"I figure if those men have to walk home," Orrin said, "It might cool their tempers some."

A slow half hour passed before one of the men down below got ambitious. My rifle put a bullet so close it must have singed his whiskers and he hunkered down in the rocks. Funny part of it was, we could see them plain as day. Had we wanted to kill them we could have. And then we heard a horse coming through the trees and I walked back to meet Torres.

"What happens, _señor?_" He looked sharply from Orrin to me.

"Looks like you were expected. Orrin and me were hunting a place for ourselves and we found some tracks, and when we followed them up there were five men down there." I showed him where. Then I explained our idea about the horses and he agreed.

"It will be for me to do, *señor*."

He went off down the slope and after awhile I saw him come out of the trees, untie the horses and run them off.

When Torres rode back Orrin came up to join us. "It is much you have done for me," Torres said. "I shall not forget."

"It is nothing," I said, "one of them is Reed Carney."

"*Gracias, Señor* Sackett," Torres said. "I believed I was safe so far from the hacienda, but a man is safe nowhere."

Riding back toward Mora I kept still and let Orrin and Torres get acquainted. Torres was a solid man and I knew Orrin would like him, and Torres liked people, so the contrary was true.

Torres turned off toward the ranch and we rode on into Mora. We got down in front of the saloon and strolled inside. It took one glance to see we weren't among friends. For one thing there wasn't a Mex in the place and this was mostly a Mexican town, and there were faces I remembered from Pawnee Rock. We found a place at the bar and ordered drinks.

There must have been forty men in that saloon, a dusty, dirty lot, most of them with uncut hair over their collars, and loaded down with six-shooters and bowie knives. Fetterson was at the other end of the bar but hadn't seen us.

We finished our drinks and edged toward the door and then we came face to face with Red . . . the one my horse had knocked down at Pawnee Rock.

He started to open his mouth, but before he could say a word, Orrin clapped him on the shoulder. "Red! You old sidewinder! Come on outside and let's talk!"

Now Red was a slow-thinking man and he blinked a couple of times, trying to decide what Orrin was talking about, and we had him outside before he could yell. He started to yell but Orrin whooped with laughter and slapped Red on the back so hard it knocked all the breath out of him.

Outside the door I put my knife against his ribs and he lost all impulse to yell. I mean he steadied down some.

"Now wait a minute," he protested, "I never done you boys any harm. I was just—"

"You just walk steady," I told him, "I'm not in the mood for trouble myself. I got a backache and I don't feel up to a shooting, so don't push me."

"Who's pushing?"

"Red," Orrin said seriously, "you're the kind of a man we like to see. Handsome, upstanding . . . and alive."

"Alive!" I added, "But you'd make a handsome corpse, Red."

By now we had him out in the dark and away from his friends, and he was scared, his eyes big as pesos. He looked like a treed coon in the lanternlight.

"What you goin' to do to me?" he protested. "Look, I—"

"Red," Orrin said, "There's a fair land up north, a wide and beautiful land. It's a land with running water, clear streams, and grass hip-high to a tall elk. I tell you Red, that's a country!"

"And you know something, Red?" I put in my two-bits' worth. "We think you should see it."

"We surely do." Orrin was dead serious. "We're going to miss you if you go, Red. But Red, you stay and we won't miss you."

"You got a horse, Red?"

"Yeah, sure." He was looking from one to the other of us. "Sure, I got a horse."

"You'll like that country up north. Now it can get too hot here for a man, Red, and the atmosphere is heavy . . . there's lead in it, you know, or liable to be. We think you should get a-straddle of that cayuse of yours, Red, and keep riding until you get to Pike's Peak, or maybe Montana."

"To—to*night*?" he protested.

"Of course. All your life you've wanted to see that country up north, Red, and you just can't wait."

"I—I got to get my outfit. I—"

"Don't do it, Red." Orrin shook his head, big-eyed. "Don't you do it." He leaned closer. "*Vigilantes*, Red. *Vigilantes*."

Red jerked under my hand, and he wet his lips with his tongue. "Now, look here!" he protested.

"The climate's bad here, Red. A man's been known to die from it. Why, I know men that'd bet you wouldn't live to see daybreak."

We came to a nice little gray. "This your horse?"

He nodded.

"You get right up into the saddle, Red. No—keep your gun. If somebody should decide to shoot you, they'd want you to have your gun on to make it look right. Looks bad to shoot an unarmed man. Now don't you feel like traveling, Red?"

By this time Red may have been figuring things out, or maybe he never even got started. Anyway, he turned his horse into the street and went out of town at a fast canter.

Orrin looked at me and grinned. "Now there's a traveling man!" He looked more serious. "I never thought we'd get out of there without a shooting. That bunch was drinking

69

and they would have loved to lynch a couple of us, or shoot us."

We rode back to join Cap and Tom Sunday. "About time. Tom has been afraid he'd have to go down and pull you out from under some Settlement man," Cap said.

"What do you mean . . . Settlement man?"

"Jonathan Pritts has organized a company which he calls the Settlement Company. You can buy shares. If you don't have money you can buy them with your·gun."

Orrin had nothing to say, he never did when Pritts' name was mentioned. He just sat down on his bed and pulled off a boot.

"You know," he said reflectively, "all that talk about the country up north convinced me. I think we should all go."

Chapter X

MORA LAY quiet in the warm sun, and along the single street, nothing stirred. From the porch of the empty house in which we had been camping, I looked up the street, feeling the tautness that lay beneath the calm.

Orrin was asleep inside the house, and I was cleaning my .44 Henry. There was trouble building and we all knew it.

Fifty or sixty of the Settlement crowd were in town, and they were getting restless for something to do, but I had my own plans and didn't intend they should be ruined by a bunch of imported trouble makers.

Tom Sunday came out on the porch and stopped under the overhang where I was working on my rifle. He took out one of those thin black cigars and lighted up.

"Are you riding out today?"

"Out to the place," I said, "we've found us a place about eight or nine miles from here."

He paused and took the cigar from his mouth. "I want a place too, but first I want to see what happens here. A man with an education could get into politics and do all right out here." He walked on down the street.

Tom was no fool; he knew there was going to be a demand for some law in Mora, and he intended to be it. I knew he wouldn't take a back seat because of Orrin.

It worried me to think of what would happen when Orrin and Tom found out each wanted the same office, although I doubted if Orrin would mind too much.

When I finished cleaning my rifle I saddled up, put my blanket roll behind the saddle and got ready to ride out. Orrin crawled out of bed and came to the door.

"I'll be out later, or Cap will," he said. "I want to keep an eye on things here." He walked to the horse with me. "Tom say anything?"

"He wants to be marshal."

Orrin scowled. "Damn it, Tyrel, I was afraid of that. He'd probably make a better .marshal than me."

."There's no telling about that, but I'd say it was a tossup, Orrin, but you can win in the election. I just hate to see you two set off against each other. Tom's a good man."

Neither one of us said anything for a while, standing there in the sun, thinking about it. It was a mighty fine morning and hard to believe so much trouble was building around us.

"I've got to talk to him," Orrin said at last, "this ain't right. We've got to level with him."

All I could think of was the fact the four of us had been together two years now, and it had been a good period for all of us. I wanted nothing to happen to that. Friendships are not so many in this life, and we had put rough country behind us and kicked up some dust in our passing, and we had smelled a little powder smoke together and there's nothing binds men together like sweat and gunsmoke.

"You go ahead, Orrin. We'll talk to Tom tomorrow."

I wanted to be there when it was talked out, because Tom liked me and he trusted me. He and Orrin were too near alike in some ways, and too different in others. There was room enough for both of them, but I was quite sure that Tom would want to go first.

It took me a shade more than an hour to ride down to where we figured to start ranching. There were trees along the river there, and some good grass, and I bedded down at the mouth of the gap, in a corner among the rocks. Picketing Montana horse, I switched from boots to moccasins and scouted around, choosing the site for the house and the corrals.

The bench where the house was to be was only twenty feet above the river, but above the highest watermark. The cliff raised up behind the bench, and the location was a good one.

Peeling off my shirt, I worked through the afternoon clearing rocks and brush off the building site and pacing it off. Then I cut poles and began building a corral for our horses, for we would need that first of all.

Later, when dark began to come, I bathed in the creek and putting on my clothes, built a small fire and made coffee and chewed on some jerked beef.

After I'd eaten I dug into my saddlebags for a book and settled down to read. Time to time I'd get up and look around, or stand for a spell in the darkness away from the fire, just listening. By the time the fire was burning down I moved back from the fire and unrolled my bed. A bit of wind was blowing up and a few clouds had drifted over the stars.

Taking my rifle I went out to check on Montana horse who was close by. I shifted his picket pin a little closer and on fresh grass. There was a feel to the night that I didn't like, and I found myself wishing the boys would show up.

When I heard a sound it was faint, but Montana horse got it, too. His head came up and his ears pricked and his nostrils reached out for the smell of things. Putting a hand on his shoulder, I said, "All right, boy. You just take it easy."

Somebody was out there in the night, calling to me.

Now a man who goes rushing out into the night will sooner or later wind up with a bullet in his belly. Me, I circled around, scouting, and moving mighty easy. I had a sight more enemies in this country than friends.

It wasn't any time at all until I saw a standing horse, heard a low moan, and then I moved in. It was a man on the ground, and he was bad hurt.

"Señor!" the voice was faint. "Please . . . it is Miguel. I come to you . . . I bring you troubles."

So I scooped him off the ground and put him on his horse. "You hang on," I said. "Only a few yards."

"Men come to kill me, señor. It will be trouble for you."

"I'll talk to them," I said, "I'll read 'em from the Scriptures."

He passed out, but I got him to camp and unloaded him. He was shot all right. He'd had the hell shot out of him. There was a bullet hole in his thigh and there was another high in his right chest that had gone clean through. His clothes were soaked with blood and he was all in.

There was water by the fire so I peeled back his clothes and went to work. First off, I bathed away the blood and plugged the holes to stop the bleeding. Come daylight, if he made it, I was going to have to do more.

With the tip of my bowie I slit the hide and eased a bullet out from under the skin of his back, then bathed the wound and fixed it up as best I could. I could hear riders working their way down the country, a-hunting him. Sooner or later

72

they'd see the reflection of my fire and then I'd have to take care of that.

Moving Miguel back out of the firelight, I got him stashed away when I heard them coming, and they came with a rush.

"Hello, the fire!"

"You're talking. Speak your piece."

"We're hunting a wounded greaser. You seen him?"

"I've seen him and he's here, but you can't have him."

They rode up to the fire then and I stepped up to the edge of the light. Trouble was, one of those riders had a rifle and it was on me, and the range wasn't fifteen feet.

That rifle worried me. They had me sweating. A fast man on the draw can beat a man who has to think before he can fire, but that first shot better be good.

"It's Sackett. The kid they say is a gunfighter."

"So it's Sackett," it was a sandy-haired man with two tied-down guns like one of these here show-off gunmen, "I ain't seen none of his graveyards."

"You just ride on," I said, "Miguel is here. He stays here."

"Talking mighty big, ain't you?" That man was Charley Smith, a big man, bearded and tough, hard to handle in a difficulty it was said. The one with the rifle was thin, angular, with a bobbing Adam's apple and a shooting look to him.

"He's wounded," I said, "I'll take care of him."

"We don't want him alive," Smith said. "We want him dead. You give him to us and you're out of it."

"Sorry."

"That's all right," Sandy said, "I like it this way. I prefer it this way."

That Sandy didn't worry me as much as the man with the rifle. Although the chances were that Sandy had practiced some with those guns. Even a show-off may be pretty fast, and I had that to think about.

Of one thing I was sure. There was no talking my way out of this. I could stand by and see them kill Miguel or I could fight them.

Now I'm not a smoking man myself, but Miguel's makings had fallen from his pocket and I'd picked them up, so I got them out and started to roll a smoke and while I talked I went right on building that smoke.

What I needed was an edge, and I needed it bad. There was the man with the rifle and Charley Smith and there was this Sandy lad who fancied himself with six-shooters. There might be more back in the dark but those three I had to think about.

"Miguel," I said, and I was talking for time, "is a good man. I like him. I wouldn't interfere in any fight of his, but on the other hand, I don't like to see a wounded man shot without a chance, either."

Smith was the cagey one. He was looking around. I guessed Smith was worried about Orrin. He knew we were a team, and he knew there was four of us, and there might be, just might be, somebody out there in the dark.

Now I was doing some serious thinking. A man who holds a gun on somebody is all keyed up and ready to shoot when he first gets the drop on you, but after awhile his muscles get a little heavy, and his reactions will be a little slower. Moreover, these fellows outnumbered me three to one. They had the advantage, so they just didn't think anybody would be fool enough to tackle them. That there was against them too. It sort of made them relax mentally, if you get what I mean.

Only any move I made must be timed just right and I had to slicker them into thinking of something else.

If they killed Miguel when he was wounded in my camp, I'd never feel right again . . . even if I lived.

"Miguel," Smith said, "is one of Alvarado's men. We're running them out."

"Where's your brother?" The man with the rifle was asking. He'd had some of his attention on the shadows out there. In this place I'd have been giving them plenty of thought.

"He's around. Those boys are never far off."

"Only one bed." That was Sandy shooting off his fat mouth. "I can see it." That was the man with the two big pistols who wanted to kill me. He could make it sound mighty big, later.

Charley Smith was going to kill me because he didn't want anybody around taking a shot at him later.

Putting that cigarette between my lips I stooped down and picked up a burning twig to light it. I lifted it to my cigarette, holding it in my fingers while I had my say.

"The four of us," I said, "never spread out very far. We work together, we fight together, and we can win together."

"They ain't around," Sandy-boy said, "only one bed, only his horse and the greaser's."

Up on the hills there was a stirring in the pines and because I'd been hearing it all evening I knew it was a wind along the ridge, but they stopped talking to listen.

"I'm a Sackett," I said conversationally, "out of Tennessee. We finished a feud a couple of years ago . . . somebody from the other outfit shot a Sackett and we killed nineteen Higginses in the next sixteen years. Never stop huntin'. I got a brother named Tell Sackett . . . best gunshot ever lived."

I was just talking, and the twig was burning. Charley Smith saw it. "Hey!" he said. "You'll burn——!"

The fire touched my fingers and I yelped with pain and dropped the twig and with the same continuing movement I drew my gun and shot that rifleman out of the saddle.

Sandy was grabbing iron when I swung my gun on him and thumbed my hammer twice so it soundd like one shot and he went backwards off his horse like he'd been hit with an axe.

Swinging my gun on Smith I saw him on the ground holding his belly and Tom Sunday came riding up with a Henry rifle.

"Smartest play I ever saw," he said, watching Smith on the ground. "When I saw you lighting up I knew there had to be something . . . knowing you didn't smoke."

"Thanks, you sure picked a good time to ride up."

Sunday got down and walked over to the man who'd held the rifle. He was dead with a shot through the heart and Sandy had taken two bullets through the heart also. Sunday glanced at me. "I saw it but I still don't believe it."

Thumbing shells into my gun I walked over to Miguel. He was up on one elbow his face whiter than I'd have believed and his eyes bigger. *"Gracias, amigos,"* he whispered.

"Orrin told me you'd come out here and I was restless so I figured I'd ride out and camp with you. When I saw you in the middle of them I was trying to figure out what to do that wouldn't start them shooting at you. Then you did it."

"They'd have killed us."

"Pritts will take your helping Miguel as a declaration of war."

There was more sound out in the darkness and we pulled back out of the light of the fire. It was Cap Rountree and two of Alvarado's hands. One of them was Pete Romero, but the other was a man I didn't know.

He was a slim, knifelike man in a braided leather jacket, the most duded-up man I ever saw, but his pearl-handled six-shooter was hung for business and he had a look in his eyes that I didn't like.

His name was Chico Cruz.

Cruz walked over to the bodies and looked at them. He took out a silver dollar and placed it over the two bullet holes in Sandy's chest. He pocketed the dollar and looked at us.

"Who?"

Sunday jerked his head to indicate me. "His . . . and

75

that one too." He indicated the man with the rifle. Then he explained what had happened, not mentioning the burning twig, but the fact that I'd been covered by the rifle.

Cruz looked at me carefully and I had a feeling this was a man who enjoyed killing and who was proud of his ability with a gun. He squatted by the fire and poured a cup of coffee. It was old coffee, black and strong. Cruz seemed to like it.

Out in the darkness, helping Romero get Miguel into the saddle, I asked, "Who's he?"

"From Mexico. Torres sent for heem. He is a bad man. He has kill many times."

Cruz looked to me like one of those sleek prairie rattlers who move like lightning and kill just as easily, and there was nothing about him that I liked. Yet I could understand the don sending for him. The don was up against a fight for everything he had. It worried him, and he knew he was getting old, and he was no longer sure that he could win.

When I came back to the fire, Chico Cruz looked up at me. "It was good shooting," he said, "but I can shoot better."

Now I'm not a man to brag, but how much better can you get?

"Maybe," I said.

"Someday we might shoot together," he said, looking at me through the smoke of his cigarette.

"Someday," I said quietly, "we might."

"I shall look forward to it, *señor*."

"And I," I smiled at him, "I shall look back upon it."

Chapter XI

WE EXPECTED trouble from Pritts but it failed to show up. Orrin came out to the place and with a couple of men Don Luis loaned us and help from Cap and Tom we put a house together. It was the second day, just after work finished when we were setting around the fire that Orrin told Tom Sunday he was going after the marshal's job.

Sunday filled his cup with coffee. His mouth stiffened up a little, but he laughed. "Well, why not? You'd make a good marshal, Orrin . . . if you get the job."

"I figured you wanted it . . ." Orrin started to say, then his words trailed off as Tom Sunday waved a hand.

"Forget it. The town needs somebody and whoever gets it

will do a job. If I don't get it and you do, I'll lend a hand
. . . I promise that. And if I get it, you can help me."

Orrin looked relieved, and I knew he was, because he had
been worried about it. Only Cap looked over his coffee cup
at Tom and made no comment, and Cap was a knowing
man.

Nobody needed to be a fortuneteller to see what was happening around town. Every night there were drunken brawls
in the street, and a man had been murdered near Elizabethtown, and there had been robberies near Cimarron. It was
just a question of how long folks would put up with it.

Meanwhile we went on working on the house, got two
rooms of it up and Orrin and me set to making furniture
for them. We finished the third room on the house and
then Orrin and me rode with Cap over to the Grant where
we bought fifty head of young stuff and drove it back and
through the gap where we branded the cattle and turned
them loose.

Working hard like we had, I'd not seen much of Drusilla,
so I decided to ride over. When I came up Antonio Baca and
Chico Cruz were standing at the gate, and I could see that
Baca was on duty there. It was the first time I'd seen him
since the night he tried to knife me on the trail.

When I started to ride through the gate, he stopped me.
"What is it you want?"

"To see Don Luis," I replied.

"He is not here."

"To see the *señorita*, then."

"She does not wish to see you."

Suddenly I was mad. Yet I knew he would like nothing
better than to kill me. Also, I detected something in his
manner . . . he was insolent. He was sure of himself.

Was it because of Chico Cruz? Or could it be that the
don was growing old and Torres could not be everywhere?

"Tell the *señorita*," I said, "that I am here. She will see
me."

"It is not necessary." His eyes taunted me. "The *señorita*
is not interested in such as you."

Chico Cruz moved his shoulders from the wall and walked
slowly over. "I think," he said, "you had better do like he
say."

There was no burned-match trick to work on them, and
anyway, I wasn't looking for a fight with any of Don Luis'
people. The don had troubles of his own without me adding
to them. So I was about to ride off when I heard her voice.

"Tye!" She sounded so glad I felt a funny little jump inside me. "Tye, why are you waiting out there? Come in!"

Only I didn't come in, I just sat my horse and said, "*Señorita*, is it all right if I call here? At any time?".

"But of course, Tye!" She came to the gate and saw Baca standing there with his rifle. Her eyes flashed. "Antonio! Put that rifle down! *Señor* Sackett is our friend! He is to come and go as he wishes, do you understand?"

He turned slowly, insolently away. "*Si*," he said, "I understand."

But when he looked at me his eyes were filled with hatred and I glanced at Cruz, who lifted a hand in a careless gesture.

When we were inside, she turned on me. "Tye, why have you stayed away? Why haven't you been to see us? Grandfather misses you. And he wanted to thank you for what you did for Juan Torres, and for Miguel."

"They were my friends."

"And you are our friend."

She looked up at me, then took my hand and led me into another room and rang a little bell.

She had grown older, it seemed, in the short time since I had last seen her. She looked taller, more composed, yet she was worried too, I could see that.

"How is Don Luis?"

"Not well, Tye. My grandfather grows old. He is more than seventy, you know. I do not even know how old, but surely more than that, and he finds it difficult to ride now.

"He fears trouble with your people. He has many friends among them, but most of them resent the size of the ranch. He wants only to keep it intact for me."

"It is yours."

"Do you remember Abreu?"

"Of course."

"He is dead. Pete Romero found him dead last week, ten miles from here. He had been shot in the back by someone with a Sharps buffalo gun."

"That's too bad. He was a good man."

We drank tea together, and she told me all that had been happening. Some days now it was difficult for the don to get out of bed, and Juan Torres was often off across the ranch. Some of the men had become hard to handle and lazy. Apparently, what had happened today was not the only such thing.

Don Luis was losing his grip when he needed desperately to be strong, and his son, Drusilla's father, had long been dead.

"If there is any way that I can help, you just call on me."

She looked down at her hands and said nothing at all,

and I sort of felt guilty, although there was no reason why. There was nobody I loved so much as Drusilla, but I'd never talked of love to anybody, and didn't know how to go about it.

"There's going to be trouble at Mora," I said, "it would be well to keep your men away from there."

"I know." She paused. "Does your brother see *Señorita Pritts*?"

"Not lately." I paused, uncertain of what to say. She seemed older.

So I told her about the place we had found, and thanked her for the help of the men the don had sent to help us with the adobe bricks. Then I told her about Tom Sunday and Orrin, and she listened thoughtfully. All the Mexicans were interested in the selection of the marshal, for it was of great importance to them. His authority would be local, but there was a chance he could move into the sheriff's job and in any case, the selection of a man would mean a lot to the Mexicans who traded in Mora and who lived there, as many did.

What I was saying wasn't at all what I wanted to say, and I searched for the words I wanted and they would not come. "Dru," I said suddenly, "I wish—"

She waited but all I could do was get red in the face and look at my hands. Finally, I got up, angry with myself. "I've got to be going," I said, "only—"

"Yes?"

"Can I come back? I mean, can I come to see you often?"

She looked straight into my eyes. "Yes, you can, Tye. I wish you would."

When I rode away I was mad with myself for saying nothing more. This was the girl I wanted. I was no hand with women but most likely Drusilla considered me a man who knew a lot about women, and figured if I had anything to say, that I'd say it.

She had a right to think that, for a man who won't speak his mind at a time like that is no man at all. More than likely she would think I just didn't want to say anything. If she thought of me that way at all.

That was a gloomy ride home, and had anybody been laying for me that night I'd have been shot dead I was that preoccupied. When I rode up to the house I saw Ollie's horse tied outside.

Ollie was there, along with a man who operated a supply store in Mora. His name was Wilson. "The time is now, Orrin. You've got to come in and stay in town a few days. Charley Smith and that sandy-haired man who was with him have done a lot to rile folks around town, and they were mighty impressed the way Tyrel handled them."

"That was Tyrel, not me."

"They know that, but they say you're two of a kind. Only," . . . Ollie looked apologetically at me, "they don't figure you're as mean as your brother. I mean they like what happened out here, only they don't hold with killing."

Orrin glanced at him. "There wasn't another thing Tyrel could have done, and mighty few who could have done what he did."

"I know that, and you know it. The fact remains that these folks want law enforced against killers but without killing. The Mexicans . . . they understand the situation better than the Americans. They know that when a man takes a weapon in hand he isn't going to put it down if you hand him a bunch of roses. Men of violence only understand violence, most times."

Orrin rode into town and for two days I stayed by the place, working around. I cleared rocks using a couple of mules and a stone boat. I dragged the rocks off and piled them where they could be used later in building a stable.

Next day I rode into town, and it looked like I'd timed things dead right. There was quite a bunch gathered outside the store Ollie was running and Ollie was on the porch, and for the first time since he came out here he had a gun where you could see it.

"It's getting so a decent person can't live in this country," he was saying. "What we need is a town marshal that will send these folks packing. Somebody we can trust to do the right thing."

He paused, and there were murmurs of agreement. "Seems to me this could be a fine, decent place to live. Most of the riffraff that cause the trouble came from Las Vegas."

Across the way on the benches I could see some of the Settlement crowd loafing and watching. They weren't worried none, it seemed like it was a laughing matter with them for they'd played top dog so long, here and elsewhere.

I went on into the saloon, and Tom Sunday was there. He glanced at me, looking sour.

"I'll buy a drink," I suggested.

"And I'll take it."

He downed the one he had and the bartender filled our glasses for us.

"You Sacketts gang up on a man," Tom declared. "Orrin's got half the town working for him. Take that Ollie Shaddock. I thought he was a friend of mine."

"He is, Tom. He likes you. Only Ollie's sort of a cousin

of ours and came from the same county back in the mountains. Ollie's been in politics all his life, Tom, and he's been wanting Orrin to have a try at it."

Tom said nothing for a little while, and then he said, "If a man is going to get any place in politics he has to have education. This won't help Orrin a bit."

"He's been studying, Tom."

"Like that fool Pritts girl. All she could see was Orrin. She never even looked at you or me."

"Womenfolks pay me no mind, Tom."

"They sure gave you all their attention in Santa Fe."

"That was different." He needed cheering up, so for the first time I told him—or anybody—of what happened that day. He grinned in spite of himself.

"No wonder. Why, that story would have been all over town within an hour." He chuckled. "Orrin was quite put out."

He tossed off his drink. "Well, if he can make it, more power to him."

"No matter what, Tom," I said, "the four of us should stick together."

He shot me a hard glance and said, "I always liked you, Tye, from the first day you rode up to the outfit. And from that day I knew you were poison mean in a difficulty."

He filled his glass. I wanted to tell him to quit but he was not a man to take advice and particularly from a younger man.

"Why don't you ride back with me?" I suggested. "Cap should be out there, and we could talk it up a little."

"What are you trying to do? Get me out of town so Orrin will have a clear field?"

Maybe I got a little red around the ears. I hadn't thought anything of the kind. "Tom, you know better than that. Only if you want that job, you'd better lay off the whiskey."

"When I want your advice," he said coolly, "I'll ask for it."

"If you feel like it," I said, "ride out. I'm taking Ma out today."

He glanced at me and then he said, "Give her my best regards, Tye. Tell her I hope she will be happy there." And he meant it, too.

Tom was a proud man, but a gentleman, and a hard one to figure. I watched him standing there by the bar and remembered the nights around the campfire when he used to recite poetry and tell us stories from the works of Homer. It gave me a lost and lonely feeling to see trouble building between us, but pride and whiskey are a bad combination, and I figured it was the realization that he might not get the marshal's job that was bothering him.

"Come out, Tom, Ma will want to see you. We've talked of you so much."

He turned abruptly and walked out the door, leaving me standing there. On the porch he paused.

Some of the settlement gang were gathered around, maybe six or eight of them, the Durango Kid and Billy Mullin right out in front. And the Durango Kid sort of figured himself as a gunman.

More than anything I wanted Tom Sunday to go home and sleep it off or to ride out to our place. I knew he was on edge, in a surly mood, and Tom could be hard to get along with.

Funny thing. Ollie had worked hard to prepare the ground work all right, and Orrin had a taking way with people, and the gift of blarney if a man ever had it.

It was a funny thing that with all of that, it was Tom Sunday who elected Orrin to the marshal's job.

He did it that day there in the street. He did it right then, walking out of that door onto the porch. He was a proud and angry man, and he had a few drinks under him, and he walked right out of the door and faced the Durango Kid.

It might have been anybody. Most folks would have avoided him when he was like that, but the Kid was hunting notches for his gun. He was a lean, narrow-shouldered man of twenty-one who had a reputation for having killed three or four men up Colorado way. It was talked around that he had rustled some cows and stolen a few horses and in the Settlement outfit he was second only to Fetterson.

Anything might have happened and Tom Sunday might have gone by, but the Durango Kid saw he had been drinking and figured he had an edge. He didn't know Tom Sunday like I did.

"He wants to be marshal, Billy," the Durango Kid said it just loud enough, "I'd like to see that."

Tom Sunday faced him. Like I said, Tom was tall, and he was a handsome man, and drinking or not, he walked straight and stood straight. Tom had been an officer in the Army at one time, and that was how he looked now.

"If I become marshal," he spoke coolly, distinctly, "I shall begin by arresting you. I know you are a thief and a murderer. I shall arrest you for the murder of Martin Abreu."

How Tom knew that, I don't know, but a man needed no more than a look at the Kid's face to know Tom had called it right.

"You're a liar!" the Kid yelled. He grabbed for his gun.

82

It cleared leather, but the Durango Kid was dead when it cleared. The range was not over a dozen feet and Tom Sunday—I'd never really seen him draw before—had three bullets into the Kid with one rolling sound.

The Kid was smashed back. He staggered against the water trough and fell, hitting the edge and falling into the street.

Billy Mullin turned sharply. He didn't reach for a gun, but Tom Sunday was a deadly man when drinking. That sharp movement of Billy's cost him, because Tom saw it out of the tail of his eye and he turned and shot Billy in the belly.

I'm not saying I mightn't have done the same. I don't think I would have, but a move like that at a time like that from a man known to be an enemy of Tom's and a friend to the Kid . . . well, Tom shot him.

That crowd across the street saw it. Ollie saw it. Tom Sunday killed the Durango Kid, and Billy Mullin was in bed for a couple of months and was never the same man again after that gunshot . . . but Tom Sunday shot himself right out of consideration as a possible marshal.

The killing of the Kid . . . well, they all knew the Kid had it coming, but the shooting of Billy Mullin, thief and everything else that he was, was so offhand that it turned even Tom's friends against him.

It shouldn't have. There probably wasn't a man across the street who mightn't have done the same thing.

It was a friend of Tom's who turned his back on him that day and said, "Let's talk to Orrin Sackett about that job."

Tom Sunday heard it, and he thumbed shells into his gun and walked down the middle of the street toward the house where he'd been sharing with Orrin, Cap, and me when we were in Mora.

And that night, Tom Sunday rode away.

Chapter XII

COME SUNDAY we drove around to the house where Ma was living with the two boys and we helped her out to the buckboard Ma was all slicked out in her Sunday-go-to-meeting clothes—which meant she was dressed in black—and all set to see her new home for the first time.

Orrin, he sat in the seat alongside her to drive, and Bob

and Joe, both mounted up on Indian ponies, they brought up the rear. Cap and me, we led off.

Cap didn't say much, but I think he had a deep feeling about what we were doing. He knew how much Orrin and me had planned for this day, and how hard we had worked. Behind that rasping voice and cold way of his I think there was a lot of sentiment in Cap, although a body would never know it.

It was a mighty exciting thing at that, and we were glad the time of year was right, for the trees were green, and the meadows green, and the cattle feeding there . . . well, it looked mighty fine. And it was a good deal better house than Ma had ever lived in before.

We started down the valley, and we were all dressed for the occasion, each of us in black broadcloth, even Cap. Ollie was going to be there, and a couple of other friends, for we'd sort of figured to make it a housewarming.

The only shadow on the day was the fact that Tom Sunday wasn't there, and we wished he was . . . all of us wished it.

Tom had been one of us so long, and if Orrin and me were going to amount to something, part of the credit had to be Tom's, because he took time to teach us things, and especially me.

When we drove up through the trees, after dipping through the river, we came into our own yard and right away we saw there were folks all around, there must have been fifty people.

The first person I saw was Don Luis, and beside him, Drusilla, looking more Irish today, than Spanish. My eyes met hers across the heads of the crowd and for an instant there we were together like we had never been, and I longed to ride to her and claim her for my own.

Juan Torres was there, and Pete Romero, and Miguel. Miguel was looking a little pale around the gills yet, but he was on his own feet and looked great.

There was a meal all spread out, and music started up, and folks started dancing a fandango or whatever they call it, and Ma just sat there and cried. Orrin, he put his arm around her and we drove all the rest of the way into the yard that way, and Don Luis stepped up and offered Ma his hand, and mister, it did us proud to see her take his hand and step down, and you'd have thought she was the grandest lady ever, and not just a mountain woman from the hills back of nowhere.

Don Luis escorted her to a chair like she was a queen, and

the chair was her own old rocker, and then Don Luis spread a serape across her knees, and Ma was home.

It was quite a shindig. There was a grand meal, with a whole steer barbecued, and three or four *javelinas*, plenty of roasting ears, and all a man could want. There was a little wine but no drinking liquor. That was because of Ma, and because we wanted it to be nice for her.

Vicente Romero himself, he was there, and a couple of times I saw Chico Cruz in the crowd.

Everybody was having themselves a time when a horse splashed through the creek and Tom Sunday rode into the yard. He sat his horse looking around, and then Orrin saw him and Orrin walked over.

"Glad you could make it, Tom. It wouldn't have been right without you. Get down and step up to the table, but first come and speak to Ma. She's been asking for you."

That was all. No words, no explanations. Orrin was that way, though. He was a big man in more ways than one, and he liked Tom, and had wanted him there.

We had a fiddle going for the dancing, and Orrin took his old gee-tar and sang up some songs, and Juan Torres sang, and we had us a time. And I danced with Dru.

When I went up to her and asked her to dance, she looked right into my eyes and accepted, and then for a minute or two we danced together and we didn't say much until pausing for a bit when I looked at her and said, "I could dance like this forever . . . with you."

She looked at me and said, her eyes sparkling a little, "I think you'd get very hungry!"

Ollie was there and he talked to Don Luis, and he talked to Torres, and he got Torres and Jim Carpenter together, and got them both with Al Brooks. They talked it over, and Torres said the Mexicans would support Orrin, and right then and there, Orrin got the appointment.

Orrin, he walked over to me and we shook hands. "We did it, Tyrel," Orrin said, "we did it. Ma's got herself a home and the boys will have a better chance out here."

"Without guns, I hope."

Orrin looked at me. "I hope so, too. Times are changing, Tyrel."

The evening passed and folks packed into their rigs or got back into the saddle and everybody went home, and Ma went inside and saw her house.

We'd bought things, the sort of things Ma would like, and some we'd heard her speak of. An old grandfather's clock, a real dresser, some fine tables and chairs, and a big old

85

four-poster bed. The house only had three rooms, but there would be more—and we boys had slept out so much we weren't fit for a house, anyway.

I walked to her carriage with Dru, and we stood there by the wheel. "I've been happy today," I told her.

"You have brought your mother home," she said. "It is a good thing. My grandfather admires you very much, Tye. He says you are a thoughtful son and a good man."

Watching Dru drive away in that carriage it made me think of money again. It's a high card in a man's hand when he goes courting if he has money, and I had none of that. True, the place we had, belonged to Orrin and me but there was more to it than that. Land wasn't of much value those days nor even cattle. And cash money was almighty scarce.

Orrin was going to be busy, so the money question was my chore.

Orrin, he worked hard studying Blackstone. From somewhere he got a book by Montaigne and he read Plutarch's *Lives*, and subscribed to a couple of eastern papers, and he read all the political news he could find, and he rode around and talked to folks or listened to them tell about their troubles. Orrin was a good listener who was always ready to give a man a hand at whatever he was doing.

That was after. That was after the first big night when Orrin showed folks who was marshal of Mora. That was the night he took over, the night he laid down the law. And believe you me, when Orrin takes a-hold, he takes a-hold.

At sundown, Orrin came up the street wearing the badge, and the Settlement men were around, taking their time to look him over. Having a marshal was a new thing in town and to the Settlement outfit it was a good joke. They just wanted to see him move around so they could decide where to lay hold of him.

The first thing Orrin done was walk through the saloon to the back door and on the inside of the back door he tacked up a notice. Now that notice was in plain sight and what was printed there was in both Spanish and English.

No gun shall be drawn or fired within the town limits.
No brawling, fighting or boisterous conduct will be tolerated.
Drunks will be thrown in jail.
Repeat offenders will be asked to leave town.
No citizen will be molested in any way.
Racing horses or riding steers in the street is prohibited.
Every resident or visitor will be expected to show visible means of support on demand.

That last rule was pointed right at the riffraff which hung around the streets, molesting citizens, picking fights, and making a nuisance of themselves. They were a bad lot.

Bully Ben Baker had been a keel-boat man on the Missouri and the Platte and was a noted brawler. He was several inches taller than Orrin, weighed two hundred and forty pounds, and Bully Ben decided to find what the new marshal was made of.

Bully Ben wasted no time. He walked over to the notice, read it aloud, then ripped it from the door.

Orrin got to his feet.

Ben reached around, grinning cheerfully, and took a bottle from the bar, gripping it by the neck.

Orrin ignored him, picked up the notice and replaced it on the door, and then he turned around and hit Ben Baker in the belly.

When Orrin had gone by him and replaced the notice, Bully Ben had waited to see what would happen. He had lowered his bottle, for he was a man accustomed to lots of rough talk before fighting, and Orrin's punch caught him off guard right in the pit of the stomach and he gasped for breath, his knees buckling.

Coolly, Orrin hit him a chopping blow to the chin that dropped Ben to his knees. The unexpected attack was the sort of thing Ben himself had often done but he was not expecting it from Orrin.

Ben came up with a lunge, swinging his bottle and I could have told him he was a fool. Blocking the descending blow with his left forearm, Orrin chopped that left fist down to Ben's jaw. Deliberately then, he grabbed the bigger man and threw him with a rolling hip-lock. Ben landed heavily and Orrin stood back waiting for him to get up.

All this time Orrin had acted mighty casual, like he wasn't much interested. He was just giving Bully Ben a whipping without half trying.

Ben was mighty shook up and he was astonished too. The blood was dripping from a cut on his jawbone and he was stunned, but he started to get up.

Orrin let him get up and when Ben threw a punch, Orrin grabbed his wrist and threw him over his shoulder with a flying mare. This time Baker got up more slowly, for he was a heavy man and he had hit hard. Orrin waited until he was halfway to his feet and promptly knocked him down.

Ben sat on the floor staring up at Orrin. "You're a fighter," he said, "you pack a wallop in those fists."

The average man in those years knew little of fist-fighting. Men in those days, except such types as Bully Ben, never thought of fighting with anything other than a gun. Ben had won his fights because he was a big man, powerful, and had acquired a rough skill on the river boats.

Pa had taught us and taught us well. He was skilled at Cornish-style wrestling and he'd learned fist-fighting from a bare-knuckle boxer he'd met in his travels.

Ben was a mighty confused man. His strength was turned against him, and everything he did, Orrin had an answer for. On a cooler night Orrin would never have worked up a sweat.

"You had enough?" Orrin asked.

"Not yet," Ben said, and got up.

Now that was a mighty foolish thing, a sadly foolish thing, because until now, Orrin had been teaching him. Now Orrin quit fooling. As Ben Baker straightened up, Orrin hit him in the face with both fists before Ben could get set. Baker made an effort to rush and holding him with his left, Orrin smashed three wicked blows to his belly, then pushed Ben off and broke his nose with an overhand right. Ben backed up and sat down and Orrin grabbed him by the hair and picking him off the floor proceeded to smash three or four blows into his face, then Orrin picked Ben up, shoved him against the bar and said, "Give him a drink." He tossed a coin on the bar and walked out.

Looked to me like Orrin was in charge.

After that there was less trouble than a man would expect. Drunks Orrin threw in jail and in the morning he turned them out.

Orrin was quick, quiet, and he wasted no time talking. By the end of the week he had jailed two men for firing guns in the town limits and each had been fined twenty-five dollars and costs. Both had been among the crowd at Pawnee Rock and Orrin told them to get out of town or go to work.

Bob and me rode down to Ruidoso with Cap Rountree and picked up a herd of cattle I'd bought for the ranch, nigh onto a hundred head.

Ollie Shaddock hired a girl to work in his store and he devoted much of his time to talking about Orrin. He went down to Santa Fe, over to Cimarron and Elizabethtown, always on business, but each time he managed to say a few words here and there about Orrin, each time mentioning him for the legislature.

After a month of being marshal in Mora there had been no killings, only one knifing, and the Settlement crowd had mostly moved over to Elizabethtown or to Las Vegas. Folks were talking about Orrin all the way down to Socorro and Silver City.

On the Grant there had been another killing. A cousin of Abreu's had been shot . . . from the back. Two of the Mexican hands had quit to go back to Mexico.

Chico Cruz had killed a man in Las Vegas. One of the Settlement crowd.

Jonathan Pritts came up to Mora with his daughter and he bought a house there.

It was two weeks after our housewarming before I got a chance to go see Dru. She was at the door to meet me and took me in to see her grandfather. He looked mighty frail, lying there in bed.

"It is good to see you, *señor*," he said, almost whispering. "How is your ranch?"

He listened while I told him about it and nodded his head thoughtfully. We had three thousand acres of graze, and it was well-watered. A small ranch by most accounts.

"It is not enough," he said, at last, "to own property in these days. One must be strong enough to keep it. If one is not strong, then there is no hope."

"You'll be on your feet again in no time," I said.

He smiled at me, and from the way he smiled, he knew I was trying to make him feel good. Fact was, right at that time I wouldn't have bet that he'd live out the month.

Jonathan Pritts, he told me, was demanding a new survey of the Grant, claiming that the boundaries of the Grant were much smaller than the land the don claimed. It was a new way of getting at him and a troublesome one, for those old Grants were bounded by this peak or that ridge or some other peak, and the way they were written up a man could just about pick his own ridges and his own peak. If Pritts could get his own surveyor appointed they would survey Don Luis right out of his ranch, his home, and everything.

"There is going to be serious trouble," he said at last. "I shall send Drusilla to Mexico to visit until it is over."

Something seemed to go out of me right then. If she went to Mexico she would never come back because the don was not going to win his fight. Jonathan Pritts had no qualms, and would stop at nothing.

I sat there with my hat in my hand wishing I could say something, but what did I have to offer a girl like Drusilla? I was nigh to broke. Right then I was wondering what we could do for operating expenses, and it was no time to talk marriage to a girl, even if she would listen to me, when that girl was used to more than I could ever give her.

At last the don reached for my hand, but his grip was feeble. "*Señor*, you are like a son to me. We have seen too little of you, Drusilla snd I, but I have found much in you to respect, and to love. I am afriad, *señor*, that I have not long, and I am the last of my family. Only Drusilla is left. If there is anything you can do, *señor*, to help her . . . take care of her, *señor*."

"Don Luis, I'd like . . . I mean . . . I don't have any money, Don Luis. Right now I'm broke. I must get money to keep my ranch working."

"There are other things, my son. You have strength, and you have youth, and those are needed now. If I had the strength. . . ."

Drusilla and I sat at the table together in the large room, and the Indian woman served us. Looking down the table at her my heart went out to her, I wanted her so. Yet what could I do? Always there was something that stood between us.

"Don Luis tells me you are going to Mexico?"

"He wishes it. There is trouble here, Tye."

"What about Juan Torres?"

"He is not the same . . . something has happened to him, and I believe he is afraid now."

Chico Cruz . . .

"I will miss you."

"I do not want to go, but what my grandfather tells me to do, I must do. I am worried for him, but if I go perhaps he will do what must be done."

"Any way I can help?"

"No!" She said it so quickly and sharply that I knew what she meant. What had to be done we both knew: Chico Cruz must be discharged, fired, sent away. But Dru was not thinking of the necessity, she was thinking of me, and she was afraid for me.

Chico Cruz . . .

We knew each other, that one and I, and we each had a feeling about the other.

If this had to be done, then I would do it myself. There was no hope that the Don would recover in time, for we both knew that when we parted tonight we might not meet again. Don Luis did not have the strength, and his recovery would take weeks, or even months.

What was happening here I understood. Torres was afraid of Cruz and the others knew it, so their obedience was half-hearted. There was no leader here, and it was nothing Cruz had done or needed to do. I doubted if he had thought of it . . . it was simply the evil in him and his willingness to kill.

Whatever was to be done must be done now, at once, so as we ate and talked I was thinking it out. This was nothing for Orrin, Cap, or anyone but me, and I must do it tonight. I must do it before this went any further.

Perhaps then she would stay, for I knew that if she ever left I would never see her again.

At the door I took her hand . . . it was the first time I had found courage to do it. "Dru . . . do not worry. I will come to see you again." Suddenly, I said what I had been thinking. "Dru . . . I love you."

And then I walked swiftly away, my heels clicking on the pavement as I crossed the court. But I did not go to my horse, but to the room of Juan Torres.

It seemed strange that a man could change so in three years since we had met. Three years? He had changed in months. And I knew that Cruz had done this, not by threats, not by warnings, just by the constant pressure of his being here.

"Juan . . . ?"

"Señor?"

"Come with me. We are going to fire Chico Cruz."

He sat very still behind the table and looked at me, and then he got up slowly.

"You think he will go?"

He looked at me, his eyes searching mine. And I told him what I felt. "I do not care whether he goes or stays."

We walked together to the room of Antonio Baca. He was playing cards with Pete Romero and some others.

We paused outside and I said, "We will start here. You tell him."

Juan hesitated only a minute, and then he stepped into the room and I followed. "Baca, you will saddle your horse and you will leave . . . do not come back."

Baca looked at him, and then he looked at me, and I said, "You heard what Torres said. You tried it once in the dark when my back was turned. If you try it now you will not be so lucky."

He put his cards into a neat, compact pile, and for the first time he seemed at a loss. Then he said, "I will talk to Chico."

"We will talk to Chico. You will go." Taking out my watch, I said, "Torres has told you. You have five minutes."

We turned and went down the row of rooms and stopped before one that was in the dark. Torres struck a light and lit

91

a lantern. He held the light up to the window and I stepped into the door.

Chico Cruz had been sitting there in the darkness. Torres said, "We don't need you any longer, Chico, you can go ... now."

He looked at Torres from his dark, steady eyes and then at me.

"There is trouble here," I said, "and you do not make it easier."

"You are to make me go?" His eyes studied me carefully.

"It will not be necessary. You will go."

His left hand and arm were on the table, toying with a .44 cartridge. His right hand was in his lap.

"I said one day that we would meet."

"That's fool talk. Juan has said you are through. There is no job for you here, and the quarters are needed."

"I like it here."

"You will like it elsewhere." Torres spoke sharply. His courage was returning. "You will go now ... tonight."

Cruz ignored him. His dark, steady eyes were on me. "I think I shall kill you, señor."

"That's fool talk," I said casually and swung my boot up in a swift, hard kick at the near edge of the table. It flipped up and he sprang back to avoid it and tripped, falling back to the floor. Before he could grasp a gun I kicked his hand away, then grabbed him quickly by the shirt and jerked him up from the floor, taking his gun and dropping him in one swift moment.

He knew I was a man who used a gun and he expected that, but I did not want to shoot him. He clung to his wrist and stared at me, his eyes unblinking like those of a rattler.

"I told you, Cruz."

Torres walked to the bunk and began stuffing Chico's clothes into his saddlebags, and rolling his bedroll. Chico still clung to his wrist.

"If I go they will attack the hacienda," Cruz said, "is that what you want?"

"It is not. But we will risk it. We cannot risk you being here, Chico. There is an evil that comes with you."

"And not with you?" He stared at me.

"Perhaps ... anyway, I shall not be here."

We heard the sound of a horse outside, and glanced out to see Pete Romero leading Chico's horse.

Chico walked to the door and he looked at me. "What of my gun?" he said, and swung into the saddle.

"You may need it," I said, "and I would not want you without it."

So I handed him the gun, nor did I take the shells from it. He opened the loading gate and flipped the cylinder curiously, and then he looked at me and held the gun in his palm, his face expressionless.

For several seconds we remained like that, and I don't know what he was thinking. He had reason to hate me, reason to kill me, but he held the gun in his hand and looked down at me, and my own gun remained in its holster.

He turned his horse. "I think we will never meet," he said, "I like you, *señor*."

Juan Torres and I stood there until we could hear the gallop of his horse no longer.

Chapter XIII

JONATHAN PRITTS had brought with him an instrument more dangerous than any gun. He brought a printing press.

In a country hungry for news and with a scarcity of reading material, the newspaper was going to be read, and people believe whatever they read must be true—or it would not be in print.

Most folks don't stop to think that the writer of a book or the publisher of a newspaper may have his own axe to grind, or he may be influenced by others, or may not be in possession of all the information on the subject of which he writes.

Don Luis had known about Pritts' printing press before anybody else, and that was one reason he wanted his granddaughter out of the country, for a paper can be used to stir people up. And things were not like they had been.

Don Luis sent for me again, and made a deal to sell me four thousand acres of his range that joined to mine. The idea was his, and he sold it to me on my note.

"It is enough, *señor*. You are a man of your word, and you can use the range." He was sitting up that day. He smiled at me. "Moreover, *señor*, it will be a piece of land they cannot take from me, and they will not try to take it from you."

At the same time, I bought, also on my note, three hundred head of young stuff. In both cases the notes were made payable to Drusilla.

The don was worried, and he was also smart. It was plain that he could expect nothing but trouble. Defeat had angered

Jonathan Pritts, and he would never quit until he had destroyed the don or been destroyed himself.

His Settlement crowd had shifted their base to Las Vegas although some of them were around Elizabethtown and Cimarron, and causing trouble in both places. But the don was playing it smart . . . land and cattle sold to me they would not try to take, and he felt sure I'd make good, and so Drusilla would have that much at least coming to her.

These days I saw mighty little of Orrin. Altogether we had a thousand or so head on the place now, mostly young stuff that would grow into money. The way I figured, I wasn't going to sell anything for another three years, and by that time I would be in a position to make some money.

Orrin, the boys, and me, we talked it over. We had no idea of running the big herds some men were handling, or trying to hold big pieces of land. All the land I used I wanted title to, and I figured it would be best to run only a few cattle, keep from overgrazing the grass, and sell fat cattle. We had already found out we could get premium prices for cattle that were in good shape.

Drusilla was gone.

The don was a little better, but there was more trouble. Squatters had moved into a valley on the east side of his property and there was trouble. Pritts jumped in with his newspaper and made a lot more of the trouble than there had been.

Then Orrin was made sheriff of the county, and he asked Tom to become a deputy.

Now we had a going ranch and everything was in hand. We needed money, and if I ever expected to make anything of myself it was time I had at it. There was nothing to do about the ranch that the boys could not do, but I had notes to Don Luis to pay and it was time I started raising some money.

Cap Rountree rode out to the ranch. He got down from his horse and sat down on the step beside me.

"Cap," I said, "you ever been to Montana?"

"Uh-huh. Good country, lots of grass, lots of mountains, lots of Indians, mighty few folks. Except around Virginia City. They've got a gold strike up there."

"That happened some years back."

"Still working." He gave me a shrewd look out of those old eyes. "You gettin' the itch, too?"

"Need money. We're in debt, Cap, and I never liked being beholden to anybody. Seems to me we might strike out north and see what we can find. You want to come along?"

"Might's well. I'm gettin' the fidgets here."

So we rode over to see Tom Sunday. Tom was drinking more than a man should. He had bought a ranch for himself about ten miles from us. He had him some good grass, a fair house, but it was a rawhide outfit, generally speaking, and not at all like Tom was who was a first-rate cattleman.

"I'll stay here," he told me finally. "Orrin offered me a job as deputy sheriff, but I'm not taking it. I think I'll run for sheriff myself, next election."

"Orrin would like to have you," I said. "It's hard to get good men."

"Hell," Tom said harshly, "he should be working for me. By rights that should be my job."

"Maybe. You had a chance at it."

He sat down at the table and stared moodily out the window.

Cap got to his feet. "Might's well come along," he said, "if you don't find any gold you'll still see some fine country."

"Thanks," he said, "I'll stay here."

We mounted up and Tom put a hand on my saddle. "Tye," he said, "I've got nothing against you. You're a good man."

"So's Orrin, Tom, and he likes you."

He ignored it. "Have a good time. If you get in trouble, write me and I'll come up and pull you out of it."

"Thanks. And if you get in trouble, you send for us."

He was still standing there on the steps when we rode away, and I looked back when I could barely make him out, but he was still standing there.

"Long as I've known him, Cap," I said, "that was the first time I ever saw Tom Sunday without a shave."

Cap glanced at me out of those cold, still eyes. "He'd cleaned his gun," he said. "He didn't forget that."

The aspen were like clusters of golden candles on the green hills, and we rode north into a changing world. "Within two weeks we'll be freezin' our ears off," Cap commented.

Nonetheless, his eyes were keen and sharp and Cap sniffed the breeze each morning like a buffalo-hunting wolf. He was a new man, and so was I. Maybe this was what I was bred for, roaming the wild country, living off it, and moving on.

In Durango we hired out and worked two weeks on a roundup crew, gathering cattle, roping and branding calves. Then we drifted west into the Abajo Mountains, sometimes called the Blues. It was a mighty big country, two-thirds of it standing on edge, seemed like. We rode through country that looked like hell with the fires out, and we camped at night among the cool pines.

Our tiny fire was the only light in a vast world of darkness, for any way we looked there was nothing but night and the stars. The smell of coffee was good, and the smell of fresh wood burning. We hadn't seen a rider for three days when we camped among the pines up there in the Blues, and we hadn't seen a track in almost as long. Excepting deer tracks, cat or bear tracks.

Out of Pioche I got a job riding shotgun for a stage line with Cap Rountree handling the ribbons. We stayed with it two months.

Only one holdup was attempted while I rode shotgun because it seemed I was a talked-about man. That one holdup didn't pan out for them because I dropped off the stage and shot the gun out of one of the outlaw's hands—it was an accident, as my foot slipped on a rock and spoiled my aim—and put two holes in the other one.

We took them back into town, and the shot one lived. He lived but he didn't learn . . . six months later they caught him stealing a horse and hung him to the frame over the nearest ranch gate.

At South Pass City we holed up to wait out a storm and I read in a newspaper how Orrin was running for the state legislature, and well spoken of. Orrin was young but it was a time for young men, and he was as old as Alexander Hamilton in 1776, and older than William Pitt when he was chancellor in England. As old as Napoleon when he completed his Italian campaign.

I'd come across a book by Jomini on Napoleon, and another by Vegetius on the tactics of the Roman legions. Most of the time I read penny dreadfuls as they were all a body could find, except once in a while those paper-bound classics given away by the Bull Durham company for coupons they enclosed. A man could find those all over the west, and many a cowhand had read all three hundred and sixty of them.

We camped along mountain streams, we fished, we hunted, we survived. Here and yonder we had a brush with Indians. One time we outran a bunch of Blackfeet, another time had a set-to with some Sioux. I got a nicked ear out of that one and Cap lost a horse, so we came into Laramie astride Montana horse, the both of us riding him.

Spring was coming and we rode north with the changing weather and staked a claim on a creek in Idaho, but nothing contented me any more. We had made our living, but little more than that. We'd taken a bunch of furs and sold out well, and I'd made a payment to Don Luis and sent some money home.

There was a two-by-four town near where we staked our claim. I mean, there was no town but a cluster of shacks and a saloon called the Rose-Marie. A big man with a square red face, sandy-red hair and small blue eyes ran the place. He laid his thick hands on the bar and you saw the scars of old fist fights there, and those little eyes studied you cruel . . . like he was figuring how much you'd be worth to him.

"What'll you have, gents? Something to cut the dust?"

"Out of that bottle in the cabinet," I said, as I'd seen him take a drink out of it himself. "We'll have a shot of that bourbon."

"I can recommend the barrel whiskey."

"I bet you can. Give it to us from the bottle."

"My own whiskey. I don't usually sell it."

There were two men sitting at a back table and they were sizing us up. One thing I'd noticed about those men. They got their service without paying. I had a hunch they worked for the firm, and if they did, what did they do?

"My name is Brady," the red-haired man said, "Martin Brady."

"Good," I said, "a man should have a name." We put our money on the bar and turned to go. "You keep that bottle handy. We tried that river whiskey before."

After three days we had only a spot or two of color. Straightening up from my pick I said, "Cap, the way I hear it we should have a burro, and when the burro strays, we follow him, and when we find that burro he's pawing pay dirt right out of the ground, or you pick up a chunk to chunk at the burro and it turns out to be pure-dee gold."

"Don't you believe all you hear." He pushed his hat back. "I been lookin' the ground over. Over there," he indicated what looked like an old stream bed, "that crick flowed for centuries. If there's gold in the crick there's more of it under that bench there."

Up on the bench we cut timber and built a flume to carry water and a sluice box. Placer mining isn't just a matter of scooping up sand and washing it out in a pan. The amount of gold a man can get that way is mighty little, and most places he can do as well punching cows or riding shotgun on a stage.

The thing to do is locate some color and then choose a likely spot like this bench and sink a shaft down to bedrock, panning out that gravel that comes off the bedrock, working down to get all the cracks and to peel off any loose slabs and work the gravel gathered beneath them. Gold is heavy, and over the years it works deeper and deeper through loose earth or gravel until it reaches bedrock and can go no further.

When we started to get down beyond six feet we commenced getting some good color, and we worked all the ground we removed from there on down. Of a night I'd often sit up late reading whatever came to hand, and gradually I was learning a good bit about a lot of things.

On the next claim there was a man named Clark who loaned me several books. Most of the reading a man could get was pretty good stuff . . . nobody wanted to carry anything else that far.

Clark came to our fire one night. "Cap, you make the best sourdough bread I ever ate. I'm going to miss it."

"You taking out?"

"She's deep enough, Cap, I'm leaving tomorrow. I'm going back to the States, to my wife and family. I worked in a store for six, seven years and always wanted one of my own."

"You be careful," Cap said.

Clark glanced around, then lowered his voice. "Have you heard those yarns, too? About the killings?"

"They found Wilton's body last week," I said, "he'd been buried in a shallow grave but the coyotes dug him out."

"I knew him." Clark accepted another plate of beans and beef and then he said, "I believe those stories. Wilton was carrying a heavy poke, and he wasn't a man to talk it around."

He forked up some more beans, then paused. "Sackett, you've been talked up as a man who's good with a gun."

"It's exaggerated."

"If you'll ride out with me I'll pay you a hundred dollars each."

"That's good money, but what about our claim?"

"This means everything to me, boys. I talked to Dickey and Wells, and they're reliable men who will watch your claim."

Cap lit up his pipe and I poured coffee for all of us. Clark just wasn't a-woofin'. Most of the miners who gambled their money away at the Rose-Marie in town had no trouble leaving. It was only those who tried to leave with their money. At least three were sitting a-top some fat pokes of gold wondering how to get out alive and still keep what they'd worked for.

"Clark," I said, "Cap and me, we need the money. We'd help even if you couldn't afford to pay."

"Believe me, it's worth it."

So I got up off the ground. "Cap, I'll just go in and have a little talk with Martin Brady."

Clark got up. "You're crazy!"

"Why, I wouldn't want him to think us deceitful, Clark, so I'll just go tell him we're riding out tomorrow. I'll also tell him what will happen if anybody bothers us."

There were thirty or forty men in the Rose-Marie when I came in. Brady came to me, drying his big hands on his apron. "We're fresh out of bourbon," he said, "you'll have to take bar whiskey."

"I just came to tell you Jim Clark is riding out of the country tomorrow and he's taking all that gold he didn't spend in here."

You could have heard a pin drop. When I spoke those words I said them out loud so everybody could hear. Brady's cigar rolled between his teeth and he got white around the eyes, but I had an eye on the two loafers at the end of the bar.

"Why tell me?" He didn't know what was coming but he knew he wouldn't like it.

"Somebody might think Clark was going alone," I said "and they might try to kill him the way Wilton and Jacks and Thompson were killed, but I figured it would be deceitful of me to ride along with Clark and let somebody get killed trying to get his gold. You see, Clark is going to make it."

"I hope he does," Brady rolled that cigar again, those cold little eyes telling me they hated me. "He's a good man."

He started to walk away but I wasn't through with him. "Brady?"

He turned slowly.

"Clark is going through because I'm going to see that he gets through, and when he's gone, I'm coming back."

"So?" He put his big hands on the edge of the bar. "What does that mean?"

"It means that if we have any trouble at all, I'm going to come back here and either run you out of town or bury you."

Somebody gasped and Martin Brady's face turned a kind of sick white, he was that mad.

"It sounds like you're calling me a thief." He kept both hands in plain sight. "You'd have to prove that."

"Prove it? Who to? Everybody knows what killing and robbery there has been was engineered by you. There's no court here but a six-shooter court and I'm presiding."

So nothing happened. It was like I figured and it was out

in the open now, and Martin Brady had to have me killed, but he didn't dare do it right then. We put Clark on the stage and started back to our own claims.

We were almost to bedrock now and we wanted to clean up and get out. We were getting the itch to go back to Santa Fe and back to Mora. Besides, I kept thinking of Dursilla.

Bob Wells was sitting on our claim with a rifle across his knees when we came in. "I was gettin' spooked," he said, "it don't seem like Brady to take this layin' down."

Dickey came over from his claim and several others, two of whom I remembered from the Rose-Marie Saloon the night I told off Martin Brady.

"We been talking it around," Dickey said, "and we figure you should be marshal."

"No."

"Can you name anybody else?" Wells asked reasonably. "This gold strike is going to play out, but a few of the mines will continue to work, and I plan to stay on here. I want to open a business, and I want this to be a clean town."

The others all pitched in, and finally Dickey said, "Sackett, with all respect, I believe it's your public duty."

Now I was beginning to see where reading can make a man trouble. Reading Locke, Hume, Jefferson, and Madison, had made me begin to think mighty high of a man's public duty.

Violence is an evil thing, but when the guns are all in the hands of the men without respect for human rights, then men are really in trouble.

It was all right for folks back east to give reasons why trouble should be handled without violence. Folks who talk about no violence are always the ones who are first to call a policeman, and usually they are sure there's one handy.

"All right," I said, "on two conditions: first, that somebody else takes over when the town is cleaned up. Second, that you raise money enough to buy out Martin Brady."

"*Buy* him out? I say, run him out!"

Who it was yelled, I don't know, but I spoke right up in meeting. "All right, whoever you are. You run him out."

There was a silence then, and when they had gathered the fact that the speaker wasn't going to offer I said, "We run him out and we're no better than he is."

"All right," Wells agreed, "buy him out."

"Well, now," I said, "we can be too hasty. I didn't say we should buy him out, what I say is we should *offer*. We make him a cash offer and whatever he does then is up to him."

Next day in town I got down from my horse in front of the store. Wind blew dust along the street and skittered dry leaves along the boardwalk. It gave me a lonesome feeling. Looking down the street I had a feeling the town would die.

No matter what happened here, what I was going to do was important. Maybe not for this town, but for men everywhere, for there must be right. Strength never made right, and it is an indecency when it is allowed to breed corruption. The west was changing. One time they would have organized vigilantes and had some necktie parties, but now they were hiring a marshal, and the next step would be a town meeting and a judge or a mayor.

Martin Brady saw me come in. His two men standing at the bar saw me too, and one of them moved a mite so his gun could be right under his hand and not under the edge of the bar.

There was nothing jumpy inside me, just a slow, measured, waiting feeling.

Around me everything seemed clearer, sharper in detail, the shadows and lights, the grain of wood on the bar, the stains left by the glasses, a slight tic on the cheek of one of Brady's men, and he was forty feet away.

"Brady, this country is growing up. Folks are moving in and they want schools, churches, and quiet towns where they can walk in the streets of an evening."

He never took his eyes from me, and I had a feeling he knew what was coming. Right then I felt sorry for Martin Brady, although his kind would outlast my kind because people have a greater tolerance for evil than for violence. If crooked gambling, thieving, and robbing are covered over, folks will tolerate it longer than outright violence, even when the violence may be cleansing.

Folks had much to say about the evil of those years, yet it took hard men to live the life, and their pleasures were apt to be rough and violent. They came from the world around, the younger sons of fine families, the ne'er-do-wells, the soldiers of fortune, the drifters, the always-broke, the promoters, the con men, the thieves. The frontier asked no questions and gave its rewards to the strong.

Maybe it needed men like Martin Brady, even the kind who lived on murder and robbery, to plant a town here at such a jumping-off place to nowhere. An odd thought occurred to me. Why had he called the saloon and the town Rose-Marie?

"Like I said, the country is growing up, Martin. You've been selling people rot-gut liquor, you've been cheating them out of hide an' hair, you've been robbing and murdering them. Murdering them was going too far, Martin, because when you start killing men, they fight back."

"What are you gettin' at, Sackett?"

"They elected me marshal."

"So?"

"You sell out, Martin Brady, they'll pay you a fair price. You sell out, and you get out."

He took the cigar from his teeth with his left hand and rested that hand on the bar. "And if I don't want to sell?"

"You have no choice."

He smiled and leaned toward me as if to say something in a low tone and when he did he touched that burning cigar to my hand.

My hand jerked and I realized the trick too late and those gunmen down the bar, who had evidently seen it done before, shot me full of holes.

My hand jerked and then guns were hammering. A slug hit me and turned me away from the bar, and two more bullets grooved the edge of the bar where I'd been standing.

Another slug hit me and I started to fall but my gun was out and I rolled over on the floor with bullets kicking splinters at my eyes and shot the big one with the dark eyes.

He was coming up to me for a finishing shot and I put a bullet into his brisket and saw him stop dead still, turn half around and fall.

Then I was rolling over and on my feet and out of the corner of my eye I saw Martin Brady standing with both hands on the bar and his cigar in his teeth, watching me. My shirt was smoldering where it had caught fire from that black powder, but I shot the other man, taking my time, and my second bullet drove teeth back into his mouth and I saw the blood dribble from the corner of his mouth.

They were both down and they weren't getting up and I looked at Martin Brady and I said, "You haven't a choice, Martin."

His face turned strange and shapeless and I felt myself falling and remembered Ma asking me about Long Higgins.

There were cracks in the ceiling. It seemed I lay there staring at them for a dozen years, and remembered that it had been a long time since I'd been in a house and wondered if I was delirious.

Cap Rountree came into the room and I turned my head and looked at him. "If this here is hell, they sure picked the right people for it."

"Never knew a man to find so many excuses to get out of his work," Cap grumbled. "How much longer do I do the work in this shebang?"

"You're an old pirate," I said, "who never did an honest day's work in his life."

Cap came back in with a bowl of soup which he started spooning into me. "Last time I recollect they were shooting holes in me. Did you plug them up?"

"You'll hold soup. Only maybe all your sand run out."

On my hand I could see the scar of that cigar burn, almost healed now. That was one time I was sure enough outsmarted. It was one trick Pa never told me about, and I'd had to learn it the hard way.

"You took four bullets," Cap said, "an' lost a sight more blood than a man can afford."

"What about Brady?"

"He lit a shuck whilst they were huntin' a rope to hang him." Cap sat down. "Funny thing. He showed up here the next night."

"Here?"

"Stopped by to see how you was. Said you were too good a man to die like that—both of you were damned fools but a man got into a way of livin' and there was no way but to go on."

"The others?"

"Those boys of his were shot to doll rags."

Outside the door I could see the sunshine on the creek and I could hear the water chuckling over the rocks, and I got to thinking of Ma and Drusilla, and one day when I could sit up I looked over at Cap.

"Anything left out there?"

"Ain't been a day's wages in weeks. If you figure to do any more minin' you better find yourself another crick."

"We'll go home. Come morning you saddle up."

He looked at me skeptically. "Can you set a saddle?"

"If I'm going home. I can sit a saddle if I'm headed for Santa Fe."

Next morning, Cap and me headed as due south as the country would allow, but it is a long way in the saddle from Idaho to New Mexico.

From time to time we heard news about Sacketts. Men on the trail carried news along with them and everybody was on the prod to know all that was going on. The Sackett news was all Orrin . . . it would take awhile for the story of what happened at Rose-Marie to get around and I'd as soon it never did. But Orrin was making a name for himself. Only there was a rumor that he was to be married.

Cap told me that because he heard it before I did and neither of us made comments. Cap felt as I did about Laura Pritts and we were afraid it was her.

We rode right to the ranch.

Bob came out to meet us, and Joe was right behind him. Ma had seen us coming up the road.

She came to the steps to meet me. Ma was better than she had been in years, a credit to few worries and a better climate, I suppose. There was a Navajo woman helping with the housework now, and for the first time Ma had it easier.

There were bookshelves in the parlor and both the boys had taken to reading.

There was other news. Don Luis was dead . . . had been buried only two days ago, but already the Settlement crowd had moved in. Torres was in bad shape . . . he had been ambushed months ago and from what I was told there was small chance he'd be himself again.

Drusilla was in town.

And Orrin was married to Laura Pritts.

Chapter XIV

ORRIN CAME out to the ranch in the morning, driving a buckboard. He got down and came to me with his hand out, a handsome man by any standards, wearing black broadcloth now like he was born to it.

He was older, more sure of himself, and there was a tone of authority in his voice. Orrin had done all right, no doubt of that, and beneath it all he was the same man he had always been, only a better man because of the education he had given himself and the experience behind him.

"It's good to see you, boy." He was sizing me up as he talked, and I had to grin, for I knew his way.

"You've had trouble," he said suddenly, "you've been hurt."

So I told him about Martin Brady and the Rose-Marie, my brief term as marshal, and the showdown.

When he realized how close I'd come to cashing in my chips he grew a little pale. "Tyrel," he said slowly, "I know what you've been through, but they need a man right here. They need a deputy sheriff who is honest and I sure know you'd never draw on anybody without cause."

"Has somebody been saying the contrary?" I asked him quietly.

"No . . . no, of course not." He spoke hastily, and I knew he didn't want to say who, which was all the answer I needed.

"Of course, there's always talk about a man who has to use a gun. Folks don't understand."

He paused. "I suppose you know I'm married?"

"Heard about it. Has Laura been out to see Ma?"

Orrin flushed. "Laura doesn't take to Ma. Says a woman smoking is indecent, and smoking a pipe is worse."

"That may be true," I replied carefully. "Out here you don't see it much, but that's Ma."

He kicked at the earth, his face gloomy. "You may think I did wrong, Tyrel, but I love that girl. She's . . . she's different, Tyrel, she's so pretty, so delicate, so refined and everything. A man in politics, he needs a wife like that. And whatever else you can say about Jonathan, he's done everything he could to help me."

I'll bet, I said to myself. I'll just bet he has. And he'll want a return on it too. So far I hadn't noticed Jonathan Pritts being freehanded with anything but other folks' land.

"Orrin, if Laura suits you, and if she makes you happy, then it doesn't matter who likes her. A man has to live his own life."

Orrin walked out to the corral with me and leaned on the rail and we stood there and talked the sun out of the sky and the first stars up before we went in to dinner. He had learned a lot, and he had been elected to the legislature, and a good part of it had been the Mexican vote, but at the last minute the Pritts crowd had gotten behind him, too. He had won by a big majority and in politics a man who can command votes can be mighty important.

Already they were talking about Orrin for the United States Senate, or even for governor. Looking at him across the table as he talked to Ma and the boys, I could see him as a senator . . . and he'd make a good one.

Orrin was a smart man who had grown smarter. He had no illusions about how a man got office or kept it, yet he was an honest man, seeking nothing for himself beyond what he could make in the natural way of things.

"I wanted Tom Sunday for the deputy job," Orrin said, "he turned it down, saying he didn't need any handouts." Orrin looked at me. "Tye, I didn't mean it that way. I liked Tom, and I needed a strong man here."

"Tom could have handled it," Cap said. "That's bad, Tom feelin' thataway."

Orrin nodded. "It doesn't seem right without Tom. He's changed, Cap. He drinks too much, but that's only part of it. He's like an old bear with a sore tooth, and I'm afraid there'll be a killing if it keeps up."

Orrin looked at me. "Tom always liked you. If there is

105

anybody can keep him in line it will be you. If anybody else even tried, and that includes me, he would go for his gun."

"All right."

Miguel rode over on the second day and we talked. Drusilla did not want to see me—he'd been sent to tell me that.

"Why, Miguel?"

"Because of the woman your brother has married. The *señorita* believes the hatred of Jonathan Pritts killed her father."

"I am not my brother's keeper," I replied slowly, "nor did I choose his wife." I looked up at him. "Miguel, I love the *señorita*."

"I know, *señor*. I know."

The ranch was moving nicely. The stock we had bought had fattened out nicely, and some had been sold that year.

Bill Sexton was sheriff, and I took to him right off, but I could also see that he was an office man, built for a swivel chair and a roll-top desk.

Around Mora I was a known man, and there was mighty little trouble. Once I had to run down a couple of horse thieves, but I brought them in, without shooting, after trailing them to where they had holed up, then—after they'd turned in—I Injuned down there and got their guns before I woke them up.

Only once did I see Tom Sunday. He came into town, unshaven and looking might unpleasant, but when he saw me he grinned and held out his hand. We talked a few minutes and had coffee together, and it seemed like old times.

"One thing," he said, "you don't have to worry about. Reed Carney is dead."

"What happened?"

"Chico Cruz killed him over to Socorro."

It gave me a cold feeling, all of a sudden, knowing that gun-slinging Mexican was still around, and I found myself hoping that he did not come up this way.

When I'd been on the job about a week I was out to the ranch one day when I saw that shining black buckboard coming, only it wasn't Orrin driving. It was Laura.

I walked down from the steps to meet her. "How are you, Laura? It's good to see you."

"It isn't good to see you." She spoke sharply, and her lips thinned down. Right at that moment she was a downright ugly woman. "If you have any feeling for your brother, you will leave here and never come back!"

"This is my home."

"You'd better leave," she insisted, "everybody knows you're a vicious killer, and now you've wheedled the deputy's

106

job out of Sexton, and you'll stay around here until you've ruined Orrin and me and everybody."

She made me mad so I said, "What's the difference between being a killer and hiring your killing done."

She struck at me, but I just stepped back and she almost fell out of the buckboard. Catching her arm, I steadied her, and she jerked away from me. "If you don't leave, I'll find a way to make you. You hate me and my father and if it hadn't been for you there wouldn't have been any of this trouble."

"I'm sorry. I'm staying."

She turned so sharply that she almost upset the buggy and drove away, and I couldn't help wondering if Orrin had ever seen her look like that. She wasn't like that hammer-headed roan I'd said she was like. That roan was a whole damned sight better.

Ma said nothing to me but I could see that she missed Orrin's visits, which became fewer and fewer. Laura usually contrived to have something important to do or somewhere important for him to be whenever he thought about coming out.

There was talk of rustling by Ed Fry who ranched near Tom's place, and we had several complaints about Tom Sunday. Whatever else Tom might be, he was an honest man. I got up on Kelly and rode the big red horse out to Sunday's place.

It was a rawhide outfit. I mean it the western way where a term like that is used to mean an outfit that's held together with rawhide, otherwise it would fall apart.

Tom Sunday came to the door when I rode up and he stood leaning against the doorjamb watching me tie my horse.

"That's a good horse, Tye," he said, "you always had a feeling for a good horse."

He squatted on his heels and began to build a smoke. Hunkering down beside him I made talk about the range and finally asked him about his trouble with Fry.

He stared at me from hard eyes. "Look, Tye, that's my business. You leave it alone."

"I'm the law, Tom," I said mildly. "I want to keep the peace if I can do it."

"I don't need any help and I don't want any interference."

"Look, Tom, look at it this way. I like this job. The boys do all there is to do on the ranch, so I took this job. If you make trouble for me, I may lose out."

His eyes glinted a little with sardonic humor. "Don't try to get around me, Tye. You came down here because you've

107

been hearing stories about me and you're worried. Well, the stories are a damned lie and you know it."

"I do know it, Tom, but there's others."

"The hell with them."

"That may be all right for you, but it isn't for me. One reason I came down was to check on what's been happening, another was to see you. We four were mighty close for a long time, Tom, and we should stay that way."

He stared out gloomily. "I never did get along with that high-and-mighty brother of yours, Tye. He always thought he was better than anybody else."

"You forget, Tom. You helped him along. You helped him with his reading, almost as much as you did me. If he is getting somewhere it is partly because of you."

I figured that would please him but it didn't seem to reach him at all. He threw his cigarette down. "I got some coffee," he said, and straightening up he went inside.

We didn't talk much over coffee, but just sat there together, and I think we both enjoyed it. Often on the drives we would ride for miles like that, never saying a word, but with a kind of companionship better than any words.

There was a book lying on the table called *Bleak House* by Charles Dickens. I'd read parts of some of Dickens' books that were run as serials in papers. "How is it?" I asked.

"Good . . . damned good."

He sat down opposite me and tasted the coffee. "Seems a long time ago," he said gloomily, "when you rode up to our camp outside of Baxter Springs."

"Five years," I agreed. "We've been friends a long time, Tom. We missed you, Cap and me, on this last trip."

"Cap and you are all right. It's that brother of yours I don't like. But he'll make it all right," he added grudgingly, "he'll get ahead and make the rest of us look like bums."

"He offered you a job. That was the deal: if you won you were to give him a job, if he won he would give you a job."

Tom turned sharply around. "I don't need his damned job! Hell, if it hadn't been for me he'd never have had the idea of running for office!"

Now that wasn't true but I didn't want to argue, so after awhile I got up and rinsed out my cup. "I'll be riding. Come out to the house and see us, Tom. Cap would like to see you and so would Ma." Then I added, "Orrin isn't there very much."

Tom's eyes glinted. "That wife of his. You sure had her figured right. Why, if I ever saw a double-crossing no-account female, she's the one. And her old man . . . I hate his guts."

When I stepped into the saddle I turned for one last word. "Tom, stay clear of Ed Fry, will you? I don't want trouble."

"You're one to talk." He grinned at me. "All right, I'll lay off, but he sticks in my craw."

Then as I rode away, he said, "My respects to your mother, Tye."

Riding away I felt mighty miserable, like I'd lost something good out of my life. Tom Sunday's eyes had been bloodshot, he was unshaven and he was careless about everything but his range. Riding over it, I could see that whatever else Tom might be, he was still a first-rate cattleman. Ed Fry and some of the others had talked of Tom's herds increasing, but by the look of things it was no wonder, for there was good grass, and he was keeping it from overgrazing, which Fry nor the others gave no thought to . . . and his water holes were cleaned out, and at one place he'd built a dam in the river to stop water so there would be plenty to last.

There was no rain. As the months went by, the rains held off, and the ranchers were worried, yet Tom Sunday's stock, in the few times I rode that way, always looked good. He had done a lot of work for a man whose home place was in such rawhide shape, and there was a good bit of water dammed up in several washes, and spreader dams he had put in had used the water he had gotten to better effect, so he had better grass than almost anybody around.

Ed Fry was a sorehead. A dozen times I'd met such men, the kind who get something in their craw and can't let it alone. Fry was an ex-soldier who had never seen combat, and was a man with little fighting experience anywhere else, and in this country, a man who wasn't prepared to back his mouth with action was better off if he kept still. But Ed Fry was a big man who talked big, and was too egotistical to believe anything could happen to him.

One morning when I came into the office I sat down and said, "Bill, you could do us both a favor if you'd have a talk with Ed Fry."

Sexton put down some papers and rolled his cigar in his jaws. "Has he been shooting off his mouth again?"

"He sure has. It came to me secondhand, but he called Tom Sunday a thief last night. If Tom hears about that we'll have a shooting. In fact, if Cap Rountree heard it there would be a shooting."

Sexton glanced at me. "And I wouldn't want you to hear it," he said bluntly, "or Orrin, either."

"If I figured to do anything about it, I'd take off this badge. There's no place in this office for personal feelings."

Sexton studied the matter. "I'll talk to Ed. Although I

don't believe he'll listen. He only gets more bullheaded. He said the investigation you made was a cover-up for Sunday, and both you and Orrin are protecting him."

"He's a liar and nobody knows it better than you, Bill. When he wants to bear down, Tom Sunday is the best cattleman around. Drunk or sober he's a better cattleman than Ed Fry will ever be."

Sexton ran his fingers through his hair. "Tye, let's make Ed put up or shut up. Let's demand to know what cattle he thinks he has missing, and what, exactly, makes him suspect Sunday. Let's make him put his cards on the table."

"You do it," I said, "he would be apt to say the wrong thing to me. The man's a fool, talking around the way he is."

Since taking over my job as deputy sheriff and holding down that of town marshal as well, I'd not had to use my gun nor had there been a shooting in town in that time. I wanted that record to stand, but what concerned me most was keeping Tom Sunday out of trouble.

Only sometimes there isn't anything a man can do, and Ed Fry was a man bound and determined to have his say. When he said it once too often it was in the St. James Hotel up at Cimarron, and there was quite a crowd in the saloon.

Clay Allison was there, having a drink with a man from whom he was buying a team of mules. That man was Tom Sunday.

Cap was there, and Cap saw it all. Cap Rountree had a suspicion that trouble was heading for Sunday when he found out that Fry was going to Cimarron. Cap already knew that Sunday had gone there, so he took off himself, and he swapped horses a couple of times but beat Fry to town.

Ed Fry was talking when Cap Rountree came into the St. James. "He's nothing but a damned cow thief!" Fry said loudly. "That Tom Sunday is a thief and those Sacketts protect him!"

Tom Sunday had a couple of drinks under his belt and he turned slowly and looked at Ed Fry.

Probably Fry hadn't known until then that Sunday was in the saloon, because according to the way Cap told it, Fry went kind of gray in the face and Cap said you could see the sweat break out on his face. Folks had warned him what loose talk would do, but now he was face to face with it.

Tom was very quiet. When he spoke you could hear him in every corner of the room, it was that still.

"Mr. Fry, it comes to my attention that you have on repeated occasions stated that I was a cow thief. You have done this on the wildest supposition and without one particle of evidence. You have done it partly because you are yourself a poor cowman as well as a very inept and stupid man."

When Tom was drinking he was apt to fall into a very precise way of speaking as well as using all that highfalutin language he knew so well.

"You can't talk to me like—"

"You have said I was a cow thief, and you have said the Sacketts protect me. I have never been a cow thief, Mr. Fry, and I have never stolen anything in my life, nor do I need protection from the Sacketts or anyone else. Anyone that says I have stolen cattle or that I have been protected is a liar, Mr. Fry, a very fat-headed and stupid liar."

He had not raised his voice but there was something in his tone that lashed a man like a whip and in even the simplest words, the way Tom said them, there was an insult.

Ed Fry lunged to his feet and Tom merely watched him. "By the Lord—"

Ed Fry grabbed for his gun. He was a big man but a clumsy one, and when he got the gun out he almost dropped it. Sunday did not make a move until Fry recovered his grip on the gun and started to bring it level, and then Tom palmed his gun and shot him dead.

Cap Rountree told Bill Sexton, Orrin, and me about it in the sheriff's office two days later. "No man ever had a better chance," Cap said, "Tom, he just stood there and I figured for a minute he was going to let Fry kill him. Tom's fast, Tye, he's real fast."

And the way he looked at me when he said it was a thing I'll never forget.

Chapter XV

IT WAS ONLY a few days later that I rode over to see Drusilla.

Not that I hadn't wanted to see her before, but there had been no chance. This time there was nobody to turn me away and I stopped before an open doorway.

She was standing there, tall and quiet, and at the moment I appeared in the door she turned her head and saw me.

"Dru," I said, "I love you."

She caught her breath sharply and started to turn away. "Please," she said, "go away. You mustn't say that."

When I came on into the room she turned to face me.

"Tye, you shouldn't have come here, and you shouldn't say that to me."

"You know that I mean it?"

She nodded. "Yes . . . I know. But you love your brother, and his wife's family hate me, and I . . . I hate them too."

"If you hate them, you're going about it as if you tried to please them. They think they've beaten your grandfather and beaten you because you live like a hermit. What you should do is come out, let people see you, go to places."

"You may be right."

"Dru, what's happening to you? What are you going to do with yourself? I came here today to pay you money, but I'm glad I came and for another reason.

"Don Luis is gone, and he was a good man, but he would want you to be happy. You are a beautiful girl, Dru, and you have friends. Your very presence around Santa Fe would worry Laura and Jonathan Pritts more than anything we could think of. Besides, I want to take you dancing. I want to marry you, Dru."

Her eyes were soft. "Tye, I've always wanted to marry you. A long time ago I would have done it had you asked me, that first time you visisted us in Santa Fe. . . ."

"I didn't have anything. I was nobody. Just another drifter with a horse and a gun."

"You were you, Tye."

"Sometimes there were things I wanted to say so bad I'd almost choke. Only I never could find the words."

So we sat down and we had coffee again like we used to and I told her about Laura and Ma, which made Dru angry.

"There's trouble shaping, Dru. I can't read the sign clear enough to say where it will happen, but Pritts is getting ready for a showdown.

"There's a lot could happen, but when it happens, I want you with me."

We talked the sun down, and it wasn't until I got up to go that I remembered the money.

She pushed it away. "No, Tyrel, you keep if for me. Invest it for me if you want to. Grandfather left me quite a bit, and I don't know what to do with it now."

That made sense, and I didn't argue with her. Then she told me something that should have tipped me off as to what was coming.

"I have an uncle, Tye, and he is an attorney. He is going to bring an action to clear the titles to all the land in our Grant. When they are clear," she added, "I am going to see the United States Marshal moves any squatters off the land."

Well . . . what could I say? Certainly it was what needed to be done and what had to be done sooner or later, but there was nothing I could think of that was apt to start more trouble than that.

Jonathan Pritts had settled a lot of his crowd on land belonging to the Alvarado Grant. Then he had bought their claims from them, and he was now laying claim to more than a hundred thousand acres. Probably Pritts figured when the don died that he had no more worries . . . anyway, he was in it up to his ears and if the title of the Alvarado Grant proved itself, he had no more claim than nothing. I mean, he was broke.

Not that I felt sorry for him. He hadn't worried about what happened to the don or his granddaughter, all he thought of was what he wanted. Only if there was anything that was figured to blow the lid off this country it was such a suit.

"If I were you," I advised her, "I'd go to Mexico and I'd stay there until this is settled."

"This is my home," Dru said quietly.

"Dru, you don't seem to realize. This is a shooting matter. They'll kill you . . . or they'll try."

"They may try," she said quietly. "I shall not leave."

When I left the house I was worried about Dru. If I had not been so concerned with her situation I might have given some thought to myself.

They would think I had put her up to it.

From the day that action was announced I would be the Number-One target in the shooting gallery.

When I was expecting everything to happen, nothing happened. There were a few scattered killings further north. One was a Settlement man who had broken with Jonathan Pritts and the Settlement Company . . . it was out of my bailiwick and the killing went unsolved, but it had an ugly look to it.

Jonathan Pritts remained in Santa Fe, Laura was receiving important guests at her parties and fandangos most every night. Pritts was generally agreed to have a good deal of political power. Me, I was a skeptic . . . because folks associate in a social way doesn't mean they are political friends, and most everybody likes a get-together.

One Saturday afternoon Orrin pulled up alongside me in a buckboard. He looked up at me and grinned as I sat Sate's saddle.

"Looks to me like you'd sell that horse, Tyrel," he said. "He was always a mean one."

"I like him," I said. "He's contrary as all get-out, and he's got a streak of meanness in him, but I like him."

"How's Ma?"

"She's doing fine." It was a hot day and the sweat trickled down my face. The long street was busy. Fetterson was down there with the one they called Paisano, because he gave a man a feeling that he was some kin to a chaparral cock or road runner. Folks down New Mexico way called them *paisanos*.

Only I had a feeling about Paisano. I didn't care for him much.

"Ma misses you, Orrin. You should drive out to see her."

"I know . . . I know. Damn it, Tyrel, why can't womenfolks get along?"

"Ma hasn't had any trouble with anybody. She's all right, Orrin, the same as always. Only she still smokes a pipe."

He mopped his face, looking mighty harried and miserable. "Laura's not used to that." He scowled. "She raises hell every time I go out to the place."

"Womenfolks," I said, "sometimes need some handling. You let them keep the bit in their teeth and they'll make you miserable and themselves too. You pet 'em a little and keep a firm hand on the bridle and you'll have no trouble."

He stared down the sun-bright street, squinting his eyes a little. "It sounds very easy, Tyrel. Only there's so many things tied in with it. When we become a state I want to run for the Senate, and it may be only a few years now."

"How do you and Pritts get along?"

Orrin gathered the reins. He didn't need to tell me. Orrin was an easygoing man, but he wasn't a man you could push around or take advantage of. Except maybe by that woman.

"We don't." He looked up at me. "That's between us, Tyrel. I wouldn't even tell Ma. Jonathan and I don't get along, and Laura . . . well, she can be difficult."

"You were quite a bronc rider, Orrin."

"What's that mean?"

"Why," I pushed my hat back on my head, "I'd say it meant your feet aren't tied to the stirrups, Orrin. I'd say there isn't a thing to keep you in the saddle but your mind to stay there, and nobody's going to give you a medal for staying in the saddle when you can't make a decent ride of it.

"Take Sate here," I rubbed Sate's neck and that bronc laid back his ears, "you take Sate. He's a mean horse. He's tough and he's game and he'll go until the sun comes up, but Orrin, if I could only have one horse, I'd never have this one. I'd have Dapple or that Montana horse.

"It's fun to ride a mean one when you don't have to do it every day, but if I stay with Sate long enough he'll turn on me. And there's some women like that."

Orrin gathered the reins. "Too hot . . . I'll see you later, Tyrel."

He drove off and I watched him go. He was a fine, upstanding man but when he married that Laura girl he bought himself a packet of grief.

Glancing down the street I saw Fetterson hand something to Paisano. It caught the sunlight an instant, then disappeared in Paisano's pocket. But the glimpse was enough. Paisano had gotten himself a fistful of gold coins from Fetterson, which was an interesting thought.

Sometimes a man knows something is about to happen. He can't put a finger on a reason, but he gets an itch inside him, and I had it now.

Something was building up. I could smell trouble in the making, and oddly enough it might have been avoided by a casual comment. The trouble was that I did not know that Torres was coming up from Socorro, and that he was returning to work for Dru.

Had I known that, I would have known what Jonathan Pritts' reaction was to be.

If Dru had happened to mention the fact that Torres was finally well and able to be around and was coming back, I would have gone down to meet him and come back with him.

Juan Torres was riding with two other Mexicans, men he had recruited in Socorro to work for Dru, and they were riding together. They had just ridden through the gap about four miles from Mora when they were shot to doll rags.

Mountain air is clear, and sound carries, particularly when it has the hills behind it. The valley was narrow all the way to town, and it was early monring with no other sound to interfere.

Orrin had come up from Santa Fe by stage to Las Vegas and had driven up to town from there. We had walked out on the street together for I'd spent the night in the back room at the sheriff's office.

We all heard the shots, there was a broken volley that sounded like four or five guns at least, and then, almost a full half minute later, a single, final shot.

Now nobody shoots like that if they are hunting game. For that much shooting it has to be a battle, and I headed for Orrin's buckboard on the run with him right behind

115

me. His Winchester was there and each of us wore a belt gun.

Dust lingered in the air at the gap, only a faint suggestion of it. The killers were gone and nobody was going to catch up with them right away, especially in a buckboard, so I wasted no time thinking about that.

Juan Torres lay on his back with three bullet holes in his chest and a fourth between his eyes, and there was a nasty powder burn around that.

"You know what that means?" I asked Orrin.

"Somebody wanted him dead. Remember that final shot?"

There was a rattle of hoofs on the road and I looked around to see my brother Joe and Cap Rountree riding bareback. The ranch was closer than the town and they must have come as fast as they could get to their horses.

They knew better than to mess things up.

Juan Torres had been dead when that final shot was fired, I figured, because at least two of the bullets in the chest would have killed him. The two others were also dead.

I began casting for sign. Not thirty feet off the trail I found where several men had waited for quite some time. There were cigarette stubs there and the grass was matted down.

Orrin had taken one look at the bodies and had walked back to the buckboard and he stood there, saying no word to anybody, just staring first at the ground and then at his hands, looking like he'd never seen them before.

A Mexican I knew had come down the road from town, and he was sitting there on his horse looking at those bodies.

"*Bandidos*?" he looked at me with eyes that held no question.

"No," I said, "assassins."

He nodded his head slowly. "There will be much trouble," he said, "this one," he indicated Torres, "was a good man."

"He was my friend."

"*Si*."

Leaving the Mexican to guard the road approaching the spot—just beyond the gap—I put Joe between the spot and the town. Only I did this after we loaded the bodies in the buckboard. Then I sent Orrin and Cap off to town with the bodies.

Joe looked at me, his eyes large. "Keep anybody from messing up the road," I said, "until I've looked it over."

First I went back to the spot in the grass where the dry-gulchers had waited. I took time to look all around very carefully before approaching the spot itself.

Yet even as I looked, a part of my mind was thinking this

116

would mean the lid was going to blow off. Juan Torres had been a popular man and he had been killed, the others, God rest their souls, were incidental. But it was not that alone, it was what was going to happen to my own family, and what Orrin already knew. Only one man had real reason to want Juan Torres dead. . . .

One of the men had smoked his cigarettes right down to the nub. There was a place where he had knelt to take aim, the spot where his knee had been and where his boot toe dug in was mighty close. He was a man, I calculated, not over five feet-four or-five. A short man who smoked his cigarettes to the nub wasn't much to go on, but it was a beginning.

One thing I knew. This had been a cold-blooded murder of men who had had no chance to defend themselves, and it had happened in my bailiwick and I did not plan to rest until I had every man who took part in it . . . no matter where the trail led.

It was a crime on my threshold, and it was a friend of mine who had been killed. And once before Orrin and I had prevented his murder . . . and another time Torres had been shot up and left for dead.

I was going to get every man Jack of them.

There had been five of them here and they had gathered up all the shells before leaving . . . or had they?

Working through the tall grass that had been crashed down by them, I found a shell and I struck gold. It was a .44 shell and it was brand, spanking new. I put that shell in my pocket with a mental note to give some time to it later.

Five men . . . and Torres himself had been hit by four bullets. Even allowing that some of them might-have gotten off more than one shot, judging by the bodies there had been at least nine shots fired before that final shot.

Now some men can lever and fire a rifle mighty fast, but it was unlikely you'd find more than one man, at most two, who could work a lever and aim a shot as fast as those bullets had been, in one group of five men.

Torres must have been moving, maybe falling after that first volley, yet somebody had gotten more bullets into him. The answer to that one was simple. There were more than five.

Thoughtfully, I looked up at that hill crested with cedar which arose behind the place where they'd been waiting. They would have had a lookout up there, someone to tell them when Torres was coming.

For a couple of hours I scouted around. I found where they had their horses and they had seven of them, and atop the ridge I found where two men had waited, smoking.

One of them had slid right down to the horses, and a man could see where he had dug his heels into the bank to keep from sliding too fast.

Cap came and lent me a hand and after a bit, Orrin came out and joined us.

One more thing I knew by that time. The man who had walked up to Torres' body and fired that last shot into his head had been a tall man with fairly new boots and he had stepped in the blood.

Although Orrin held off and let me do it—knowing too many feet would tramp everything up—he saw enough to know here was a plain, outright murder, and a carefully planned murder at that.

First off, I had to decide whether they expected to be chased or not and about how far they would run. How well did they know the country? Were they likely to go to some ranch owned by friends, or hide out in the hills?

Cap had brought back Kelly all saddled and ready, so when I'd seen about all I could see there, I got into the saddle and sent Joe back to our ranch. He was mighty upset, wanting to go along with a posse, but if it was possible I wanted to keep Joe and Bob out of any shooting and away from the trouble.

"What do you think, Tyrel?" Orrin watched me carefully as he spoke.

"It was out-and-out murder," I said, "by seven men who knew Torres would be coming to Mora. It was planned murder, with the men getting there six to seven hours beforehand. Two of them came along later and I'd guess they watched Torres from the hills to make sure he didn't turn off or stop."

Orrin stared at the backs of his hands and I didn't say anything about what I suspected nor did Cap.

"All right," Orrin said, "you go after them and bring them in, no matter how long it takes or what money you need."

I hesitated. Only Cap, Orrin, and me were there together. "Orrin," I said, "you had me hired, and you can fire me. You can leave it to Bill Sexton or you can put in someone else."

Orrin seldom got mad but he was angry when he stared back at me. "Tyrel, that's damn-fool talk. You do what you were hired to do."

Not one of the three of us could have doubted where that trail would lead, but maybe even then Orrin figured it would lead to Fetterson, maybe, but not to Pritts.

Bill Sexton came up just then. "You'll be wanting a posse," he said, "I can get a few good men."

"No posse . . . I want Cap, that's all."

"Are you crazy? There's seven of them . . . at least."

"Look, if I take a posse there's apt to be one in the crowd who's trigger happy. If I can avoid it I don't want any shooting. If I can take these men alive, I'm going to do it."

"You're looking to lose your scalp," Sexton said doubtfully, "but it's your hair. You do what you've a mind to."

"Want me to come along?" Orrin asked.

"No." I wanted him the worst way but the less involved he was, the better. "Cap will do."

The way I looked at it, the chances were almighty slim that the seven would stay together very long. Some of them would split off and that would shorten the odds.

The Alvarado Ranch lay quiet under low gray clouds when Cap and I rode up to the door. Briefly, I told Miguel about Torres. "I will come with you," he said instantly.

"You stay here." I gave it to him straight. "They thought by killing Torres they would ruin any chance the *señorita* would have. Torres is killed but you are not. You're going to take his place, Miguel. You are going to be foreman."

He was startled. "But I—"

"You will have to protect the *señorita*," I said, "and you will have to hire at least a dozen good men. You'll have to bunch what cattle she has left and guard them. It looks to me like the killing of Juan Torres was the beginning of an attempt to put her out of business."

I went on inside, walking fast, and Dru was there to meet me. Quietly as possible, I told her about Juan Torres' death and what I had told Miguel.

"He's a good man," I said, "a better man than he knows, and this will prove it to him and to you. Give him authority and give him responsibility. You can trust him to use good judgment."

"What are you going to do?"

"Why, what a deputy sheriff has to do. I am going to run down the killers."

"And what does your brother say?"

"He says to find them, no matter what, no matter how long, and no matter who."

"Tyrel—be careful!"

That made me grin. "Why, ma'am," I said, grinning at her, "I'm the most careful man you know. Getting myself killed is the last idea in my mind . . . I want to come back to you."

She just looked at me. "You know, Dru, we've waited long enough. When I've caught these men I am going to resign and we are going to be married . . . and I'm not taking no for an answer."

Her eyes laughed at me. "Who said no?"

At the gap Cap and I picked up the trail and for several miles it gave us no trouble at all. Along here they had been riding fast, trying to put distance between themselves and pursuit.

It was a green, lovely country, with mountain meadows, the ridges crested with cedar that gave way to pine as we climbed into the foothills. We camped that night by a little stream where we could have a fire without giving our presence away.

Chances were they would be expecting a large party and if they saw us, would not recognize us. That was one reason I was riding Kelly. Usually I was up on Dapple or Montana horse, and Kelly was not likely to be known.

Cap made the coffee and sat back into the shadows. He poked sticks into the fire for a few minutes the way he did when he was getting ready to talk.

"Figured you'd want to know. Pritts has been down to see Tom Sunday."

I burned my mouth on a spoonful of stew and when I'd swallowed it I looked at him and said, *Pritts to see Tom?*"

"Uh-huh. Dropped by sort of casual-like, but stayed some time."

"Tom tell you that?"

"No . . . I've got a friend down thataway."

"What happened?"

"Well, seems they talked quite some time and when Pritts left, Tom came out to the horse with him and they parted friendly."

Jonathan Pritts and Tom . . . it made no kind of sense. Or did it?

The more thought I gave to it the more worried I became, for Tom Sunday was a mighty changeable man, and drinking as he was, with his temper, anything might happen.

Orrin had had trouble with Pritts—of this I was certain sure—and Pritts had made a friendly visit to Tom Sunday. I didn't like the feel of it. I didn't like it at all.

Chapter XVI

THERE WAS a pale lemon glow over the eastern mountains when we killed the last coals of our fire and saddled up.

Kelly was feeling sharp and twisty, for Kelly was a trail-loving horse who could look over big country longer than any horse I ever knew, except maybe Montana horse.

Inside me there was a patience growing and I knew I was going to need it. We were riding a trail that could only bring us to trouble because the men we were seeking had friends who would not take lightly our taking them. But the job was ours to do and those times a man didn't think too much of consequences but crossed each bridge as he came to it.

It was utterly still. In this, the last hour before dawn, all was quiet. Even with my coat on, the sharp chill struck through and I shivered. There was a bad taste in my mouth and I hated the stubble on my jaws . . . I'd gotten used to shaving living in town and being an officer. It spoiled a man.

Even in the vague light we could see the lighter trail of pushed-down grass where the riders had ridden ahead of us. Suddenly, the trail dipped into a hollow in the trees and we found their camp of the night before.

They were confident, we could see that, for they had taken only the usual, normal precaution in hiding their camp, and they hadn't made any effort to conceal that they'd been there.

We took our time there for much can be learned of men at such a time, and to seek out a trail it is well to know the manner of men you seek after. If Cap Rountree and me were to fetch these men we would have to follow them a far piece.

They ate well. They had brought grub with them and there was plenty of it. At least a couple of them were drinking, for we found a bottle near the edge of the camp . . . it looked like whoever was drinking didn't want the others to know, for the bottle had been covered over with leaves.

"Fresh bottle," I said to Cap and handed it to him. He sniffed it thoughtfully. "Smells like good whiskey, not none of this here Indian whiskey."

"They don't want for anything. This outfit is traveling mighty plush."

Cap studied me carefully. "You ain't in no hurry."

"They finished their job, they'll want their pay. I want the man who pays them."

"You figured out who it'll be?"

"No . . . all I want is for these men to take me there. Twice before they tried to kill Juan and now they got him. I'm thinking they won't stop there and the only way to stop it is to get the man who pays out the money."

As I was talking a picture suddenly came to mind. It was

Fetterson passing out gold to that renegade Paisano. It was a thing to be remembered.

"Bearing west," Cap said suddenly, "I think they've taken a notion."

"Tres Ritos?"

"My guess." Cap considered it. "That drinkin' man now. Supposin' he's run out of whiskey? The way I figure, he's a man who likes his bottle and whoever is bossin' the bunch has kept him off it as much as possible.

"Drinkin' man now, he gets mighty canny about hidin' his stuff. He figures he got folks fooled . . . trouble is, it becomes mighty obvious to everybody but the one drinkin'. They may believe that because the job's finished they can have a drink, and Tres Ritos is the closest place."

"I'd guess it's about an easy two-hour ride from here," I looked ahead, searching out the way the riders had gone. "They've taken themselves a notion, all right. Tres Ritos, it is."

Nevertheless, we kept a close watch on the trail. Neither of us had a good feeling about it. A man living in wild country develops a sense of the rightness of things . . . and he becomes like an animal in sensing when all is not well.

So far it had been easy, but I was riding rifle in hand now and ready for trouble. Believe me, I wanted that Henry where I could use it. We had seven tough men ahead of us, men who had killed and who did not wish to be caught. I believe we had them fooled, for they would expect to be followed by a posse, but only a fool depends on a feeling like that.

Against such men you never ride easy in the saddle, you make your plans, you figure things out, and then you are careful. I never knew a really brave man yet who was reckless, nor did I ever know a real fighting man who was reckless . . . maybe because the reckless ones were all dead.

Cap drew up. "I think I'll have a smoke," he said. Cap got down from his saddle, keeping his rifle in his hand.

He drew his horse back under the trees out of sight and I did likewise. Only one fault with Kelly. That big red horse stood out like a forest fire in this green country.

We sat there studying the country around but doing no talking until Cap smoked his pipe out. Meanwhile both of us had seen a long bench far above the trail that led in the direction of Tres Ritos.

"We might ride along there," I suggested, "I'm spooky about that trail ahead."

"If they turn off we'll lose 'em."

"We can come back and pick up the trail."

We started off at an easy lope, going up through the trees, cutting back around some rocks. We'd gone about a mile when Cap pointed with his rifle.

Down the hill, not far off the trail, we could see some horses tied in the trees. One of them was a dark roan that had a familiar look. Reminded me of a horse I'd seen Paisano riding. And Paisano had taken money from Fetterson. This trail might take us somewhere at that.

We dusted the trail into Tres Ritos shy of sundown. We had taken our own time scouting around and getting the country in our minds.

We headed for the livery stable. The sleepy hostler was sitting on the ground with his back to the wall. He had a red headband and looked like a Navajo. He took our horses and we watched him stall them and put corn in the box. Cap walked down between the rows of stalls and said, "Nobody . . . we beat 'em to town."

The barkeep in the saloon was an unwashed half-breed with a scar over his left eye like somebody had clouted him with an axe.

We asked for coffee and he turned and yelled something at a back door. The girl his yell brought out was Tina Fernandez. She knew me all right. All those Santa Fe women knew me.

Only she didn't make out like she knew me. She was neat as a new pin, and she brought a pot of coffee and two cups and she poured the coffee and whispered something that sounded like *cuidado*—a word meaning we should be careful.

We drank our coffee and ate some chili and beans with tortillas and I watched the kitchen door and Cap watched the street.

The grub was good, the coffee better, so we had another cup. "Behind the corral," she whispered, "after dark."

Cap chewed his gray mustache and looked at me out of those old, wise-hard eyes. "You mixin' pleasure with business?"

"This is business."

We finished our coffee and we got up and I paid the bartender while Cap studied the street outside. The bartender looked at my face very carefully and then he said, "Do I know you?"

"If you do," I said, "you're going to develop a mighty bad memory."

The street was empty. Not even a stray dog appeared. Had we guessed wrong? Had they gone around Tres Ritos? Or were they here now, waiting for us?

Standing there in the quiet of early evening I had a dry

mouth and could feel my heart beating big inside of me. Time to time I'd seen a few men shot and had no idea to go out that way if I could avoid it.

We heard them come into town about an hour later. Chances are they grew tired of waiting for us, if that was what they had been doing. They came down the street strung out like Indians on the trail, and from where we lay in the loft over the livery stable we could not see them but we could hear their horses.

They rode directly to the saloon and got down there, talking very little. As we had ridden into Tres Ritos by a back trail they would have seen no tracks, so unless they were told by the bartender they were not likely to realize we were around.

Lying there on the hay, listening out of the back of my mind for any noise that would warn us they were coming our way, I was not thinking of them, but of Orrin, Laura, Tom Sunday, Dru, and myself. And there was a lot to think about.

Jonathan Pritts would not be talking to Tom Sunday unless there was a shady side to his talk, for Jonathan was a man who did nothing by accident. I knew Tom had no use for the man, but as far back as the night Jonathan had sent for us in Santa Fe there had been a streak of compromise in Tom. He had hesitated that night, recognizing, I think, that Jonathan was a man who was going to be a power.

What was Jonathan Pritts up to? The thought stayed with me and I worried it like a dog at a bone, trying to figure it out. Of one thing I was sure: it promised no good for us.

Cap sat up finally and took out his pipe. "You're restless, boy."

"I don't like this."

"You got it to do. A man wants peace in a country he has to go straight to the heart of things." He smoked in silence for a few minutes. "Time to time I've come across a few men like Pritts . . . once set on a trail they can't see anything but that and the more they're balked the stiffer they get." He paused a moment. "As he gets older he gets meaner . . . he wants what he's after and he knows time is short."

The loft smelled of the fresh hay and of the horses below in their stalls. The sound of their eating was a comfortable sound, a good sleeping sound, but I could not sleep, tired as I was.

If I was to do anything with my life it had to be now and when this trail had been followed to the end I was going

124

to quit my job, marry Dru, and settle down to build something.

We'd never rightly had a real home and for my youngsters I wanted one. I wanted a place they could grow up with, where they could put down roots. I wanted a place they'd be proud to come back to and which they could always call home . . . no matter how far they went or what happened.

Getting up I brushed off the hay, hitched my gun belt into position, and started for the ladder.

"You be careful."

"I'm a careful man by nature."

At the back of the corral I squatted on my heels against a corral post and waited.

Time dragged and then I heard a soft rustle of feet in the grass and saw a shadow near me and smelled a faint touch of woman-smell.

"You all right?"

It was scarcely a whisper but she came to me and I stood up keeping myself in line with that corral post at the corner.

"They are gone," Tina said.

"*What?*"

"They are gone," she repeated, "I was 'fraid for you."

She explained there had been horses for them hidden in ths woods back of the saloon, and while they were inside drinking, their saddles had been switched and they had come out one by one and gone off into the woods.

"Fooled us . . . hornswoggled us."

"The other one is there. He is upstairs but I think he will go in the morning."

"Who?"

"The man who gave them money. The blond man."

Fetterson? It could be.

"You saw the money paid?"

"Yes, *señor*. With my two eyes I saw it. They were paid much in gold . . . the balance, he said."

"Tina, they killed Juan Torres . . . did you know him?"

"*Si* . . . he was a good man."

"In court, Tina. Would you testify against them? Would you tell you saw money paid? It would be dangerous for you."

"I will testify. I am not afraid." She stood very still in the darkness. "I know, *señor*, you are in love with the *Señorita* Alvarado, but could you help me, *señor*? Could you help me to go away from here? This man, the one you talked to, he is my . . . how do you call it? He married my mother."

125

"Stepfather."

"*Si* . . . and my mother is dead and he keeps me here and I work, *señor*. Someday I will be old. I wish now to go to Santa Fe again but he will not let me."

"You shall go. I promise it."

The men had gone and we had not seen them but she told me one had been Paisano. Only one other she knew. A stocky, very tough man named Jim Dwyer . . . he had been among those at Pawnee Rock. But Fetterson was here and he was the one I wanted most.

We slept a little, and shy of daybreak we rolled out and brushed off the hay. I felt sticky and dirty and wanted a bath and a shave the worst way but I checked my gun and we walked down to the hotel. There was a light in the kitchen and we shoved open the back door.

The bartender was there in his undershirt and pants and sock feet. There was the tumbled, dirty bedding where he had slept, some scattered boots, dirty socks, and some coats hung on the wall, on one nail a gun belt hung. I turned the cylinder and shucked out the shells while the bartender watched grimly.

"What's all this about?"

Turning him around we walked through the dark hall with a lantern in Cap's hand to throw a vague light ahead.

"Which room is he in?"

The bartender just looked at me, and Cap, winking at me, said, "Shall I do it here? Or should we take him out back where they won't find the body so soon?"

The bartender's feet shifted. "No, look!" he protested. "I ain't done nothing."

"He'd be in the way," I said thoughtfully, "and he's no account to us. We might as well take him out back."

Cap looked mean enough to do it, and folks always figured after a look at me that killing would be easier for me than smiling.

"Wait a minute . . . he ain't nothin' to me. He's in Room Six, up the stairs."

Looking at him, I said "Cap, you keep him here." And then looking at the bartender I said, "You know something? That had better be the right room."

Up the stairs I went, tiptoeing each step and at the top, shielding the lantern with my coat, I walked down the hall and opened the door to Room Six.

His eyes opened when I came through the door but the light was in his eyes when I suddenly unveiled the lantern and his gun was on the table alongside the bed. He started to reach for it and I said, "Go ahead, Fetterson, you pick it up and I can kill you."

His hand hung suspended above the gun and slowly he withdrew it. He sat up in bed then, a big, rawboned man with a shock of rumpled blond hair and his hard-boned, wedgelike face. There was nothing soft about his eyes.

"Sackett? I might have expected it would be you." Careful to make no mistakes he reached for the makings and began to build a smoke. "What do you want?"

"It's a murder charge, Fett. If you have a good lawyer you might beat it, but you make a wrong move and nothing will beat what I give you."

He struck a match and lit up. "All right . . . I'm no Reed Carney and if I had a chance I'd try shooting it out, but if that gun stuck in the holster I'd be a dead man."

"You'd never get a hand on it, Fett."

"You takin' me in?"

"Uh-huh. Get into your clothes."

He took his time dressing and I didn't hurry him. I figured if I gave him time he would decide it was best to ride along and go to jail, for with Pritts to back him there was small chance he would ever come to trial. My case was mighty light on evidence, largely on what Tina could tell us and what I had seen myself, which was little enough.

When he was dressed he walked ahead of me down the hall to where Cap was waiting with a gun on the bartender. We gathered up Fetterson's horse and started back to town. I wasn't through with that crowd I'd trailed, but they would have to wait.

Our return trip took us mighty little time because I was edgy about being on the trail, knowing that the bartender might get word to Fetterson's crowd. By noon the next day we had him behind bars in Mora and the town was boiling.

Fetterson stood with his hands on the bars. "I won't be here long," he said, "I'd nothing to do with this."

"You paid them off. You paid Paisano an advance earlier."

There was a tic in his eyelid, that little jump of the lid that I'd noticed long ago in Abilene when he had realized they were boxed and could do nothing without being killed.

"You take it easy," I said, "because by the time this case comes to court I'll have enough to hang you."

He laughed, and it was a hard, contemptuous laugh, too. "You'll never see the day!" he said. "This is a put-up job."

When I walked outside in the sunlight, Jonathan Pritts was getting down from his buckboard.

One thing I could say for Jonathan . . . he moved fast.

Chapter XVII

IT HAD BEEN a long time since I'd stood face to face
with Jonathan Pritts. He walked through the open door and
confronted me in the small office, his pale blue eyes hard
with anger. "You have Mr. Fetterson in prison. I want
him released."

"Sorry."

"On what charge are you holding him?"

"He is involved in the murder of Juan Torres."

He glared at me. "You have arrested this man because
of your hatred for me. He is completely innocent and you
can have no evidence to warrant holding him. If you do
not release him I will have you removed from office."

He had no idea how empty that threat was. He was a
man who liked power and could not have understood how
little I wanted the job I had, or how eager I was to be rid of
it.

"He will be held for trial."

Jonathan Pritts measured me carefully. "I see you are
not disposed to be reasonable." His tone was quieter.

"There has been a crime committed, Mr. Pritts. You
cannot expect me to release a prisoner because the first
citizen who walks into my office asks me to. The time has
come to end crimes of violence, and especially," I added
this carefully, "murder that has been paid for."

This would hit him where he lived, I thought, and maybe
it did, only there was no trace of feeling on his face. "Now
what do you mean by that?"

"We have evidence that Fetterson paid money to the
murderers of Juan Torres."

Sure, I was bluffing. We had nothing that would stand
up in court, not much, actually, on which to hold him. Only
that I had seen him paying money to Paisano, and he had
been at Tres Ritos when the killers arrived, and that Tina
would testify to the fact that he had paid money there.

"That is impossible."

Picking up a sheaf of papers, I began sorting them. He
was a man who demanded attention and my action made
him furious.

"Mr. Pritts," I said, "I believe you are involved in this
crime. If the evidence will substantiate my belief you will

hang also, right along with Fetterson and the others."

Why, he fooled me. I expected him to burst out with some kind of attack on me, but he did nothing of the kind.

"Have you talked to your brother about this?"

"He knows I have my duty to do, and he would not interfere. Nor would I interfere in his business."

"How much is the bail for Mr. Fetterson?"

"You know I couldn't make any ruling. The judge does that. But there's no bail for murder."

He did not threaten me or make any reply at all, he just turned and went outside. If he had guessed how little I had in the way of evidence he would have just sat still and waited. But I have a feeling about this sort of thing . . . if you push such men they are apt to move too fast, move without planning, and so they'll make mistakes.

Bill Sexton came in, and Ollie was with him. They looked worried.

"How much of a case have you got against Fetterson?" Sexton asked me.

"Time comes, I'll have a case."

Sexton rubbed his jaw and then took out a cigar. He studied it while I watched him, knowing what was coming and amused by all the preliminaries, but kind of irritated by them, too.

"This Fetterson," Sexton said, "is mighty close to Jonathan Pritts. It would be a bad idea to try to stick him with these killings. He's got proof he wasn't anywhere around when they took place."

"There's something to that Tye," Ollie said. "It was Jonathan who helped put Orrin in office."

"You know something?" I had my feet on the desk and I took them down and sat up in that swivel chair. "He did nothing of the kind. He jumped on the band wagon when he saw Orrin was a cinch to win. Fetterson stays in jail or I resign."

"That's final?" Ollie asked.

"You know it is."

He looked relieved, I thought. Ollie Shaddock was a good man, mostly, and once an issue was faced he would stand pat and I was doing what we both believed to be right.

"All right," Sexton said, "if you think you've got a case, we'll go along."

It was nigh to dark when Cap came back to the office. There was no light in the office and sitting back in my chair I'd been doing some thinking.

Cap squatted against the wall and lit his pipe. "There's a man in town," he said, "name of Wilson. He's a man who likes his bottle. He's showing quite a bit of money, and a few days ago he was broke."

"Pretty sky," I said, "the man who named the Sangre de Cristos must have seen them like this. That red in the sky and on the peaks . . . it looks like blood."

"He's getting drunk," Cap said.

Letting my chair down to an even keel I got up and opened the door that shut off the cells from the office. Walking over to the bars and stopping there, I watched Fetterson lying on his cot. I could not see his face, only the dark bulk of him and his boots. Yes, and the glow of his cigarette.

"When do you want to eat?"

He swung his boots to the floor. "Any time. Suit yourself."

"All right." I turned to go and then let him have it easy. "You know a man named Wilson?"

He took the cigarette from his mouth. "Can't place him. Should I?"

"You should . . . he drinks too much. Really likes that bottle. Some folks should never be trusted with money."

When I'd closed the door behind me Cap lit the lamp. "A man who's got something to hide," Cap said, "has something to worry about."

Fetterson would not, could not know what Wilson might say, and a man's imagination can work overtime. What was it the Good Book said? "The guilty flee when no man pursueth."

The hardest thing was to wait. In that cell Fetterson was thinking things over and he was going to get mighty restless. And Jonathan Pritts had made no request to see him. Was Jonathan shaping up to cut the strings on Fetterson and leave him to shift for himself? If I could think of that, it was likely Fetterson could too.

Cap stayed at the jail and I walked down to the eating house for a meal. Tom Sunday came in. He was a big man and he filled the door with his shoulders and height. He was unshaved and he looked like he'd been on the bottle. Once inside he blinked at the brightness of the room a moment or two before he saw me and then he crossed to my table. Maybe he weaved a mite in walking . . . I wouldn't have sworn to it.

"So you got Fetterson?" He grinned at me, his eyes faintly taunting. "Now that you've got him, what will you do with him?"

"Convict him of complicity," I replied. "We know he paid the money."

"That's hitting close to home," Sunday's voice held a suggestion of a sneer. "What'll your brother say to that?"

"It doesn't matter what he says," I told him, "but it happens it has been said. I cut wood and let the chips fall where they may."

"That would be like him," he said, "the sanctimonious son-of-a-bitch."

"Tom," I said quietly, "that term could apply to both of us. We're brothers, you know."

He looked at me, and for a moment there I thought he was going to let it stand, and inside me I was praying he would not. I wanted no fight with Tom Sunday.

"Sorry," he said, "I forgot myself. Hell," he said then, "we don't want trouble. We've been through too much together."

"That's the way I feel," I said, "and Tom, you can take my say-so or not, but Orrin likes you, too."

"Likes me?" he sneered openly now. "He likes me, all right, likes me out of the way. Why, when I met him he could scarcely read or write . . . I taught him. He knew I figured to run for office and he moved right in ahead of me, and you helping him."

"There was room for both of you. There still is."

"The hell there is. Anything I tried to do he would block me. Next time he runs for office he won't have the backing of Jonathan Pritts. I can tell you that."

"It doesn't really matter."

Tom laughed sardonically. "Look, kid, I'll tip you to something right now. Without Pritts backing him Orrin wouldn't have been elected . . . and Pritts is fed up."

"You seem to know a lot about Pritts' plans."

He chuckled. "I know he's fed up, and so is Laura. They're both through with Orrin, you wait and see."

"Tom, the four of us were mighty close back there a while. Take it from me, Tom, Orrin has never disliked you. Sure, the two of you wanted some of the same things but he would have helped you as you did him."

He ate in silence for a moment or two, and then he said, "I have nothing against you, Tye, nothing at all."

After that we didn't say anything for a while. I think both of us were sort of reaching out to the other, for there had been much between us, we had shared violence and struggle and it is a deep tie. Yet when he got up to leave I think we both felt a sadness, for there was something missing.

He went outside and stood in the street a minute and I

felt mighty bad. He was a good man, but nobody can buck liquor and a grudge and hope to come out of it all right. And Jonathan Pritts was talking to him.

I arrested Wilson that night. I didn't take him to jail where Fetterson could talk to him. I took him to that house at the edge of town where Cap, Orrin, and me had camped when we first came up to Mora.

I stashed him there with Cap to mount guard and keep the bottle away. Joe came in to guard Fetterson and I mounted up and took to the woods, and I wasn't riding on any wild-goose chase . . . Miguel had told me that a couple of men were camped on the edge of town, and one of them was Paisano.

From the ridge back of their camp I studied the layout through a field glass. It was a mighty cozy little place among boulders and pines that a man might have passed by fifty times without seeing had it not been for Miguel being told of it by one of the Mexicans.

The other man must be Jim Dwyer—a short, thickset man who squatted on his heels most of the time and never was without his rifle.

There was no hurry. There was an idea in my skull to the effect these men were camping here for the purpose of breaking Fetterson out of jail. I wanted those men the worst way but I wanted them alive, and that would be hard to handle as both men were tough, game men who wouldn't back up from a shooting fight.

There was a spring about fifty yards away, out of sight of the camp. From the layout I'd an idea this place had been used by them before. There was a crude brush shelter built to use a couple of big boulders that formed its walls. All the rest of the day I lay there watching them. From time to time one of them would get up and stroll out to the thin trail that led down toward Mora.

They had plenty of grub and a couple of bottles but neither of them did much drinking.

By the time dark settled down I knew every rock, every tree, and every bit of cover in that area. Also I had spotted the easiest places to move quietly in the dark, studying the ground for sticks, finding openings in the brush.

Those men down there were mighty touchy folks with whom a man only made one mistake.

Come nightfall I moved my horse to fresh grass after watering him at the creek. Then I took a mite of grub and a canteen and worked my way down to within about a hundred feet of their camp.

They had a small fire going, and coffee on. They were broiling some beef, too, and it smelled almighty good. There I was, lying on my belly smelling that good grub and chewing on a dry sandwich that had been packed early in the day. From where I lay I could hear them but couldn't make out the words.

My idea was that with Fetterson in jail it was just a chance Jonathan Pritts might come out himself.

He was a cagey man and smart enough to keep at least one man between himself and any gun trouble. But Pritts wanted Fetterson out of jail.

It seemed to me that in the time I'd known Jonathan Pritts he had put faith in nobody. Such a man was unlikely to have confidence in Fetterson's willingness to remain silent when by talking he might save his own skin. Right now I thought Pritts would be a worried man, and with reason enough.

Fetterson had plenty to think about too. He knew that we had Wilson, and Wilson was a drinker who would do almost anything for his bottle. If Wilson talked, Fetterson was in trouble. His one chance to get out of it easier was to talk himself. Personally, I did not believe Fetterson would talk —there was a loyalty in the man, and a kind of iron in him, that would not allow him to break or be broken.

I was counting on the fact that Pritts believed in nobody, was eternally suspicious and would expect betrayal.

What I did not expect was the alternative on which Jonathan Pritts had decided. I should have guessed, but did not. Jonathan was a hard man, a cold man, a resolute man.

Now it can be mighty miserable lying up in the brush, never really sleeping, and keeping an eye on a camp like that. Down there, they'd sleep awhile and then rouse up and throw some sticks on the fire, and go back to sleep again. And that's how the night run away.

It got to be the hour of dawn with the sun some time away but crimson streaking the sky, and those New Mexico sunrises . . . well, there's nothing like the way they build a glory in the sky.

Paisano stood up suddenly. He was listening. He was lower in the canyon and might hear more than I.

Would it be Jonathan Pritts himself? If it was, I would move in, taking the three of them in a bundle. Now that might offer a man a problem, and I wanted them all alive, which would not be a simple thing. Yet I had it to do.

What made me turn my head, I don't know.

There was a man standing in the brush about fifty feet

away, standing death-still, his outline vague in the shadowy brush. How long that man had been there I had no idea, but there he was, standing silent and watching.

It gave me a spooky feeling to realize that man had been so close all the while and I'd known nothing about it. Not one time in a thousand could that happen to me. Trouble was, I'd had my eyes on that camp, waiting, watching to miss nothing.

Suddenly, that dark figure in the brush moved ever so slightly, edging forward. He was higher than I, and could see down the canyon, although he was not concealed nearly so well as I was. My rifle was ready, but what I wanted was the bunch of them, and all alive so they could testify. And I'd had my fill of killing and had never wished to use my gun against anyone.

It was growing lighter, and the man in the brush was out further in the open, looking down as if about to move down there into the camp. And then he turned his head and some of the light fell across his face and I saw who it was.

It was Orrin.

Chapter XVIII

ORRIN....

It was so unexpected that I just lay there staring and then I began to bring my thoughts together and when I considered it I couldn't believe it. Sure, Orrin was married to Pritts' daughter, but Orrin had always seemed the sort of man who couldn't be influenced against his principles. We'd been closer even than most brothers.

So where did that leave me? Our lives had been built tightly around our blood ties for Lord knows how many years. Only I knew that even if it was Orrin, I was going to arrest him. Brother or not, blood tie or not, It was my job and I would do it.

And then I had another thought. Sure, I could see then I was a fool. There had to be another reason. My faith in Orrin went far beyond any suspicion his presence here seemed to mean.

So I got up.

His attention was on that camp as mine had been, and I had taken three steps before he saw me.

He turned his head and we looked into each other's eyes, and then I walked on toward him.

Before I could speak he lifted a hand. "Wait!" he whispered, and in the stillness that followed I heard what those men down below must have heard some time before . . . the sound of a buckboard coming.

We stood there with the sky blushing rose and red and the gold cresting the far-off ridges and the shadows still lying black in the hollows.

We stood together there, as we had stood together before, against the Higginses, against the dark demons of drought and stones that plagued our hillside farm in Tennessee, against the Utes, and against Reed Carney. We stood together, and in that moment I suddenly knew why he was here, and knew before the buckboard came into sight just who I would see.

The buckboard came into the trail below and drew up. And the driver was Laura.

Paisano and Dwyer went out to meet her and we watched money pass between them and watched them unload supplies from the back of the buckboard.

Somehow I'd never figured on a woman, least of all, Laura. In the west in those years we respected our women, and it was not in me to arrest one although I surely had no doubts that a woman could be mighty evil and wrong.

Least of all could I arrest Laura. It was a duty I had, but it was her father I wanted and the truth was plain to see. A man who would send his daughter on such a job . . . he was lower than I figured.

Of course, there were mighty few would believe it or even suspect such a frail, blond, and ladylike girl of meeting and delivering money to murderers.

Orrin shifted his feet slightly and sighed. I never saw him look the way he did, his face looking sick and empty like somebody had hit him in the midsection with a stiff punch.

"I had to see it," he said to me, "I had to see it myself to believe it. Last night I suspected something like this, but I had to be here to see."

"You knew where the camp was?"

"Jonathan gave her most careful directions last night."

"I should arrest her," I said.

"As you think best."

"It isn't her I want," I said, "and she would be no good to me. She'd never talk."

Orrin was quiet and then he said, "I think I'll move out to the ranch, Tyrel. I'll move out today."

135

"Ma will like that. She's getting feeble, Orrin."

We went back into the brush a mite and Orrin rolled a smoke and lit up. "Tyrel," he said after a minute, "what's he paying them for? Was it for Torres?"

"Not for Torres," I said, "Fetterson already paid them."

"For you?"

"Maybe . . . I doubt it."

Suddenly I wanted to get away from there. Those two I could find when I wanted them for they were known men, and the man I had wanted had been cagey enough not to appear.

"Orrin," I said, "I've got to head Laura off. I'm not going to arrest her, I just want her to know she was seen and I know what's going on. I want them to know and to worry about it."

"Is that why you're holding Wilson apart?"

"Yes."

We went back to our horses and then we cut along the hill through the bright beauty of the morning to join the trail a mile or so beyond where Laura would be.

When she came up, for a minute I thought she would try to drive right over us, but she drew up.

She was pale, but the planes of her face had drawn down in hard lines and I never saw such hatred in a woman's eyes.

"Now you're spying on me!" There was nothing soft and delicate about her voice then, it was strident, angry.

"Not on you," I said, "on Paisano and Dwyer."

She flinched as if I'd struck her, started to speak, then pressed her lips together.

"They were in the group that killed Juan Torres," I said, "along with Wilson."

"If you believe that, why don't you arrest them? Are you afraid?"

"Just waiting . . . sometimes if a man let's a small fish be his bait he can catch bigger fish. Like you, bringing supplies and money to them. That makes you an accessory. You can be tried for aiding and abetting."

For the first time she was really scared. She was a girl who made much of position, a mighty snooty sort, if you ask me, and being arrested would just about kill her.

"You wouldn't dare!"

She said it, but she didn't believe it. She believed I would, and it scared the devil out of her.

"Your father has been buying murder too long, and there is no place for such men. Now you know."

Her face was pinched and white and there was nothing pretty about her then. "Let me pass!" she demanded bitterly.

We drew aside, and she looked at Orrin. "You were nothing when we met, and you'll be nothing again."

Orrin removed his hat, "Under the circumstances," he said gently, "you will pardon me if I remove my belongings?"

She slashed the horses with the whip and went off. Orrin's face was white as we cut over across the hills. "I'd like to be out of the house," he said, "before she gets back."

The town was quiet when I rode in. Fetterson came to the bars of his cell and stared at me when I entered. He knew I'd been away and it worried him he didn't know what I was doing.

"Paisano and Dwyer are just outside the town," I said, "and no two men are going to manage a jail delivery, but Pritts was paying them . . . what for?"

His eyes searched my face and suddenly he turned and looked at the barred window. Beyond the window, three hundred yards away, was the wooded hillside . . . and to the right, not over sixty yards off, the roof of the store.

He turned back swiftly. "Tye," he said, "you've got to get me out of here."

Fetterson was no fool and he knew that there was no trust in Jonathan Pritts. Fetterson would die before he would talk, but Pritts did not for a minute believe that. Consequently he intended that Fetterson should die before he could talk.

"Fett," I said, "It's up to you not to get in front of that window. Or," I paused and let the word hang for a minute, "you can talk and tell me the whole story."

He turned sharply away and walked back to his cot and lay down. I knew that window would worry him, Wilson would worry him, and he would worry about how much I knew.

"You might as well tell me and save your bacon," I said, "Wilson hasn't had a drink in three days and he'll tell all he knows any day now. After that we won't care about you."

Right then I went to Ceran St. Vrain. He was the most influential man in Mora, and I had Vicente Romero come in, and we had a talk. Ollie Shaddock was there, Bill Sexton, and Orrin.

"I want ten deputies," I said, "I want Ceran to pick five of them and Romero to pick the other five. I want solid, reliable men. I don't care whether they are good men with guns or not, I want substantial citizens."

They picked them and we talked the whole thing over. I laid all my cards on the table. Told them just what the situation was and I didn't beat around the bush.

Wilson was talking, all right. He had a hand in the killing

of Torres and the others and he named the other men involved, and I told them that Paisano and Dwyer were out in the hills and that I was going after them myself. I made good on my word to Tina Fernandez and got a promise from Ceran himself to go after her with a couple of his riders to back him up. He was a man respected and liked and feared.

On Jonathan Pritts I didn't pull my punches. Telling them of our meeting with him in Abilene, of our talk with him in Santa Fe, of the men waiting at Pawnee Rock, and of what he had done since. St. Vrain was an old friend to the Alvarado family . . . he knew much of what I said.

"What is it, *señor?* What do you wish to do?"

"I believe Fetterson is ready to talk." I said, "We will have Wilson, we will have Tina, and Cap's evidence as well as my own, for we trailed the killers to Tres Ritos."

"What about Mrs. Sackett?" St. Vrain asked.

Right there I hesitated. "She's a woman and I'd like to keep her out of it."

They all agreed to this and when the meeting broke up, I was to have a final talk with Fetterson.

So this was to be an end to it. There was no anger in me any more. Juan Torres was gone and another death could not bring him back. Jonathan Pritts would suffer enough to see all his schemes come to nothing, and they would, now. I knew that Vicente Romero was the most respected man in the Spanish-speaking group, and St. Vrain among the Anglos. Once they had said what they had to say, Jonathan Pritts would no longer have influence locally nor in Santa Fe.

Orrin and me, we walked back to the jail together and it was good to walk beside him, brothers in feeling as well as in blood.

"It's tough," I said to him, "I know how you felt about Laura, but Orrin, you were in love with what you thought she was. A man often creates an image of a girl in his mind but when it comes right down to it that's the only place the girl exists."

"Maybe," Orrin was gloomy, "I was never meant to be married."

We stopped in front of the sheriff's office and Cap came out to join us.

"Tom's in town," he said, "and he's drunk and spoilin' for a fight."

"We'll go talk to him," Orrin said.

Cap caught Orrin's arm. "Not you, Orrin. You'd set him off. If you see him now there'll be a shootin' sure."

"A shooting?" Orrin smiled disbelievingly. "Cap, you're
138

clean off the trail. Why, Tom's one of my best friends!"

"Look," Cap replied shortly, "you're no tenderfoot. How much common sense or reason is there behind two-thirds of the killings out here? You bump into a man and spill his drink, you say the wrong thing . . . it doesn't have to make sense."

"There's no danger from Tom," Orrin insisted quietly. "I'd stake my life on it."

"That's just what you're doing," Cap replied. "The man's not the Tom Sunday that drove cows with us. He's turned into a mighty mean man, and he's riding herd on a grudge against you. He's been living alone down there and he's been hitting the bottle."

"Cap's right." I told him, "Tom's carrying a chip on his shoulder."

"All right, I want no trouble with him or anyone."

"You got an election comin' up," Cap added. "You get in a gun battle an' a lot of folks will turn their backs on you."

Reluctantly, Orrin mounted up and rode out to the ranch, and for the first time in my life, I was glad to see him go. Things had been building toward trouble for months now, and Tom Sunday was only one small part of it, but the last thing I wanted was a gun battle between Tom and Orrin. At all costs that fight must be prevented both for their sakes and for Orrin's future.

Ollie came by the office after Orrin had left. "Pritts is down to Santa Fe," he said, "and he's getting himself nowhere. Vicente Romero has been down there, and so has St. Vrain and it looks like they put the kibosh on him."

Tina was in town and staying with Dru and we had our deposition from Wilson. I expect he was ready to get shut of the whole shebang, for at heart Wilson was not a bad man, only he was where bad company and bad liquor had taken him.

He talked about things clear back to Pawnee Rock, and we took that deposition in front of seven witnesses, three of them Mexican, and four Anglos. When the trial came up I didn't want it said that we'd beaten it out of him, but once he started talking he left nothing untold.

On Wednesday night I went to see Fetterson for I'd been staying away and giving him time to think. He looked gaunt and scared. He was a man with plenty of sand but nobody likes to be set up as Number-One target in a shooting gallery.

"Fett," I said, "I can't promise you anything but a chance in court, but the more you co-operate the better. If you want out of this cell you'd better talk."

"You're a hard man, Tyrel," he said gloomily. "You stay with a thing."

"Fett," I said, "men like you and me have had our day. Folks want to settle affairs in court now, and not with guns. Women and children coming west want to walk a street without stray bullets flying around. A man has to make peace with the times."

"If I talk I'll hang myself."

"Maybe not . . . folks are more anxious to have an end to all this trouble than to punish anybody."

He still hesitated so I left him there and went out into the cool night. Orrin was out at the ranch and better off there, and Cap Rountree was some place up the street.

Bill Shea came out of the jail house. "Take a walk if you're of a mind to, Tyrel," he suggested, "there's three of us here."

Saddling the Montana horse I rode over to see Dru. It was a desert mountain night with the sky so clear and the stars so close it looked like you could knock them down with a stick. Dru had sold the big house that lay closer to Santa Fe, and was spending most of her time in this smaller but comfortable house near Mora.

She came to the door to meet me and we walked back inside and I told her about the meeting with Romero and St. Vrain, and the situation with Fetterson.

"Move him, Tye, you must move him out of there before he is killed. It is not right to keep him there."

"I want him to talk."

"Move him," Dru insisted, "you must. Think of how you would feel if he was killed."

She was right, of course, and I'd been thinking of it. "All right," I said, "first thing in the morning."

Sometimes the most important things in a man's life are the ones he talks about least. It was that way with Dru and me. No day passed that I did not think of her much of the time, she was always with me, and even when we were together we didn't talk a lot because so much of the time there was no need for words, it was something that existed between us that we both understood.

The happiest hours of my life were those when I was riding with Dru or sitting across a table from her. And I'll always remember her face by candlelight . . . it seemed I was always seeing it that way, and soft sounds of the rustle of gowns, the tinkle of silver and glass, and Dru's voice, never raised and always exciting.

Within the thick adobe walls of the old Spanish house there was quiet, a shadowed peace that I have associated with such houses all my years. One stepped through the door

140

into another world, and left outside the trouble, confusion, and storm of the day.

"When this is over, Dru," I said, "we'll wait no longer. And it will soon be over."

"We do not need to wait." She turned from the window where we stood and looked up at me. "I am ready now."

"This must be over first, Dru. It is a thing I have to do and when it is finished I shall take off my badge and leave the public offices to Orrin."

Suddenly there was an uneasiness upon me and I said to her, "I must go."

She walked to the door with me. *"Vaya con Dios,"* she said, and she waited there until I was gone.

And that night there was trouble in town but it was not the trouble I expected.

Chapter XIX

IT HAPPENED as I left my horse in front of the saloon and stepped in for a last look around. It was after ten o'clock, and getting late for the town of Mora, and I went into the saloon and stepped into trouble.

Two men faced each other across the room and the rest were flattened against the walls.

Chico Cruz, deadly as a sidewinder, stood posed and negligent, a slight smile on his lips, his black eyes flat and without expression.

And facing him was Tom Sunday.

Big, blond, and powerful, unshaven as always these days, heavier than he used to be, but looking as solid and formidable as a blockhouse.

Neither of them saw me. Their attention was concentrated on each other and death hung in the air like the smell of lightning on a rocky hillside. As I stepped in, they drew.

With my own eyes I saw it. Saw Chico's hand flash. I had never believed a man could draw so fast, his gun came up and then he jerked queerly and his body snapped sidewise and his gun went off into the floor and Tom Sunday was walking.

Tom Sunday was walking in, gun poised. Chico was trying to get his gun up and Tom stopped and spread his legs and grimly, brutally, he fired a shot into Chico's body, and then coolly, another shot.

Chico's gun dropped, hit the floor with a thud. Chico turned and in turning his eyes met mine across the room, and he said very distinctly into the silence that followed the thundering of the guns, "It was not you."

He fell then, fell all in a piece and his hat rolled free and he lay on the floor and he was dead.

Tom Sunday turned and stared at me and his eyes were blazing with a hot, hard flame. "You want me?" he said, and the words were almost a challenge.

"It was a fair shooting, Tom," I said quietly. "I do not want you."

He pushed by me and went out of the door, and the room broke into wild talk. "Never would have believed it. . . . Fastest thing I ever saw. . . . But *Chico!*" The voice was filled with astonishment. "He killed *Chico Cruz!*"

Until that moment I had always believed that if it came to a difficulty that Orrin could take care of Tom Sunday, but I no longer believed it.

More than any of them I knew the stuff of which Orrin was made. He had a kind of nerve rarely seen, but he was no match for Tom when it came to speed. And there was a fatal weakness against him, for Orrin truly liked Tom Sunday.

And Tom?

Somehow I didn't think there was any feeling left in Tom, not for anyone, unless it was me.

The easy comradeship was gone. Tom was ingrown, bitter, hard as nails.

When Chico's body was moved out I tried to find out what started the trouble, but it was like so many bar-room fights, just sort of happened. Two, tough, edgy men and neither about to take any pushing around. Maybe it was a word, maybe a spilled drink, a push, or a brush against each other, and then guns were out and they were shooting.

Tom had ridden out of town.

Cap was sitting in the jail house with Babcock and Shea when I walked in. I could see Fetterson through the open door, so walked back to the cells.

"That right? What they're saying?"

"Tom Sunday killed Chico Cruz . . . beat him to the draw."

Fetterson shook his head unbelievingly. "I never would have believed it. I thought Chico was the fastest thing around . . . unless it was you."

Fetterson grinned suddenly. "How about you and Tom? You two still friends?"

It made me mad and I turned sharply around and he stepped back from the bars, but he was grinning when he moved back. "Well, I just asked," he said, "some folks never bought that story about you backin' Cruz down."

"Tom is my friend," I told him, "we'll always be friends."

"Maybe," he said, "maybe." He walked back to the bars. "Looks like I ain't the only one has troubles."

Outside in the dark I told Cap about it, every detail. He listened, nodding thoughtfully.

"Tyrel," Cap said, "we been friends, and trail dust is thicker'n blood, but you watch Tom Sunday. You watch him. That man's gone loco like an old buffalo bull who's left the herd."

Cap took his pipe out of his mouth and knocked out the ashes against the awning post. "Tyrel, mark my words! He's started now an' nuthin's goin' to stop him. Orrin will be next an' then you."

That night I got into the saddle and rode all the way out to the ranch to sleep, pausing only a moment at the gap where the river flowed through, remembering Juan Torres who died there. It was bloody country and time it was quieted down. Inside me I didn't want to admit that Cap was right, but I was afraid, I was very much afraid.

As if the shooting, which had nothing to do with Pritts, Alvarado, or myself, had triggered the whole situation from Santa Fe to Cimarron, the lid suddenly blew off. Maybe it was that Pritts was shrewd enough to see his own position weakening and if anything was to be done it had to be done now.

Jonathan and Laura, they moved back up to Mora and it looked like they had come to stay.

Things were shaping up for a trial of Wilson and Fetterson for the murder of Juan Torres.

We moved Fetterson to a room in an old adobe up the street that had been built for a fort. We moved him by night and the next morning we stuck a dummy up in the window of the jail. We put that dummy up just before daylight and then Cap, Orrin, and me, we took to the hills right where we knew we ought to be.

We heard the shots down the slope from us and we went down riding fast. They were wearing Sharps buffalo guns. They both fired and when we heard those two rifles talk we came down out of the higher trees and had them boxed. The Sharps buffalo was a good rifle, but it was a single shot, and we had both those men covered with Winchesters before they could get to their horses or had time to reload.

Paisano and Dwyer. Caught flat-footed and red-handed, and nothing to show for it but a couple of bullets through a dummy.

That was what broke Jonathan Pritts' back. We had four of the seven men now and within a matter of hours after, we tied up two more. That seventh man wasn't going to cause anybody any harm. Seems he got drunk one night and on the way home something scared his horse and he got bucked off and with a foot caught in the stirrup there wasn't much he could do. Somewhere along the line he'd lost his pistol and couldn't kill the horse. He was found tangled in some brush, his foot still in the stirrup, and the only way they knew him was by his boots, which were new, and his saddle and horse. A man dragged like that is no pretty sight, and he had been dead for ten to twelve hours.

Ollie came down to the sheriff's office with Bill Sexton and Vicente Romero. They were getting up a political rally and Orrin was going to speak. Several of the high mucky-mucks from Santa Fe were coming up, but this was to be Orrin's big day.

It was a good time for him to put himself forward and the stage was being set for it. There was to be a real ol' time fandango with the folks coming in from back at the forks of the creeks. Everybody was to be there and all dressed in their Sunday-go-to-meeting clothes.

In preparation for it I made the rounds and gave several of the trouble makers their walking papers. What I mean is, I told them they would enjoy Las Vegas or Socorro or Cimarron a whole sight better and why didn't they start now.

They started.

"Have you heard the talk that's going around?" Shea asked me.

"What talk?"

"It's being said that Tom Sunday is coming into town after Orrin."

"Tom Sunday and Orrin are friends," I said, "I know Tom's changed, but I don't believe he'll go that far."

"Put no faith in that line of thought, Tyrel. Believe me, the man hasn't a friend left. He's surly as a grizzly with a sore tooth, and nobody goes near him any more. The man's changed, and he works with a gun nearly every day. Folks coming by there say they can hear it almost any hour."

"Tom never thought much of Orrin as a fighter. Tom never knew him like I have."

"That isn't all." Shea put his cigar down on the edge of the desk. "There's talk about what would happen if you and Tom should meet."

Well, I was mad. I got up and walked across the office and swore. Yes, and I wasn't a swearing man.

Oddly enough, thinking back, I can't remember many gunfighters who were. Most of them I knew were sparing in the use of words as well as whiskey.

But one thing I knew: Orrin must not meet Tom Sunday. Even if Orrin beat him, Orrin would lose. A few years ago it would not have mattered that he had been in a gun battle, now it could wreck his career.

If Orrin would get out of town ... but he couldn't. He had been selected as the speaker for the big political rally and that would be just the time when Tom Sunday would be in town.

"Thanks," I said to Shea, "thanks for telling me."

Leaving Cap in charge of the office I mounted up and rode out to the ranch. Orrin was there, and we sat down and had dinner with Ma. It was good to have our feet under the same table again, and Ma brightened up and talked like her old self.

Next day was Sunday and Orrin and me decided to take Ma to church. It was a lazy morning with bright sunshine and Orrin took Ma in the buckboard and we boys rode along behind.

We wore our broadcloth suits and the four of us dressed in black made a sight walking around Ma, who was a mighty little woman among her four tall sons, and Dru was with us, standing there beside Ma and me, and I was a proud man.

It was a meeting I'll not soon forget, that one was, because when Ollie heard the family was going, he came along and stood with us at the hymn singing and the preaching.

Whether or not Orrin had heard any of the stories going round about Tom I felt it necessary to warn him. If I expected him to brush it off, I was wrong. He was dead serious about it when I explained. "But I can't leave," he added, "everybody would know why I went and if they thought I was afraid, I'd lose as many votes as if I actually fought him."

He was right, of course, so we prepared for the meeting with no happy anticipation of it, although this was to be Orrin's big day, and his biggest speech, and the one that would have him fairly launched in politics. Men were coming up from Santa Fe to hear him, all the crowd around the capital who pulled the political strings.

Everybody knew Orrin was to speak and everybody knew Tom would be there. And nothing any of us could do but wait.

Jonathan Pritts knew he had been left out and he knew it was no accident. He also knew that it was to be Orrin's big day and that Laura's cutting loose had not hurt him one bit.

Also Jonathan knew the trial was due to come off soon,

and before the attorney got through cross-examining Wilson and some of the others the whole story of his move into the Territory would be revealed. There was small chance it could be stopped, but if something were to happen to Orrin and me, if there was to be a jail delivery. . . .

He wouldn't dare.

Or would he?

Chapter XX

THE SUN was warm in the street that morning, warm even at the early hour when I rode in from the ranch. The town lay quiet and a lazy dog sprawled in the dust opened one eye and flapped his tail in a I-won't-bother-you-if-you-don't-bother-me sort of way, as I approached.

Cap Rountree looked me over carefully from those shrewd old eyes as I rode up. "You wearing war paint, boy? If you ain't, you better. I got a bad feeling about today."

Getting down from the saddle I stood beside him and watched the hills against the skyline. People were getting up all over town now, or lying there awake and thinking about the events of the day. There was to be the speaking, a band concert, and most folks would bring picnic lunches.

"I hope he stays away."

Cap stuffed his pipe with tobacco. "He'll be here."

"What happened, Cap? Where did it start?"

He leaned a thin shoulder against the awning post. "You could say it was at the burned wagons when Orrin and him had words about that money. No man likes to be put in the wrong.

"Or you could say it was back there at the camp near Baxter Springs, or maybe it was the day they were born. Sometimes men are born who just can't abide one another from the time they meet . . . don't make no rhyme nor reason, but it's so."

"They are proud men."

"Tom's gone killer, Tyrel, don't you ever forget that. It infects some men like rabies, and they keep on killing until somebody kills them."

We stood there, not talking for awhile, each of us busy with his own thoughts. What would Dru be doing about now? Rising at home, and planning her day, bathing, combing her long dark hair, having breakfast.

Turning away I went inside and started looking over the day's roundup of mail. This morning there was a letter from Tell, my oldest brother. Tell was in Virginia City, Montana, and was planning to come down and see us. Ma would be pleased, mighty pleased. It had been a sorry time since we had seen Tell.

There was a letter from that girl, too. The one we had sent the money we found in that burned wagon . . . she was coming west and wanted to meet us. The letter had been forwarded from Santa Fe where it had been for weeks . . . by this time she must be out here, or almost here.

It gave me an odd feeling to get that letter on this morning, thinking back to the trouble it had caused.

Cap came in from outside and I said, "I'm going to have coffee with Dru. You hold the fort, will you?"

"You do that, boy. You just do that."

Folks were beginning to crowd the streets now, and some were hanging out bunting and flags. Here and there a few rigs stood along the street, all with picnic baskets in the back. There were big, rawboned men in the Sunday-go-to-meeting clothes and women in fresh-washed ginghams and sunbonnets. Little boys ran and played in the streets, and their mothers scolded and called after them while little girls, starched and ribboned, looked on enviously and disdainfully.

It was good to be alive. Everything seemed to move slow today, everything seemed to take its time . . . was this the way a man felt on his last day? Was it to be my last day?

When I knocked on the door Dru answered it herself. Beyond the welcome I could see the worry.

"How's about a poor drifter begging a cup of coffee, ma'am? I was just passin' through and the place had a kindly look."

"Come in, Tye. You don't have to knock."

"Big day in town. Biggest crowd I ever saw. Why, I've seen folks from Santa Fe . . . as far as Raton or Durango."

The maid brought in the coffee and we sat at the breakfast table looking out the low-silled window over the town and the hillside and we sat talking for awhile and at last I got up and she came with me to the door. She put her hand on my sleeve. "Stay here, Tye . . . don't go."

"Got to . . . busy day today."

Folks were crowded along the street and there were wagons drawn up where the speaking was to be—with many people

147

taking their places early so they could be close enough to hear. When I got down to the office Orrin was there in his black frock coat and string tie. He grinned at me, but beyond the grin his eyes were serious. "You get up there and talk," I said, "you're the speaker of this family."

Me, I stayed at the office. Cap was out and around, nosing after news like a smart old coon dog looking up trails in the dust or the berry patches.

There was no sign of Tom Sunday, and around the jail everything was quiet. Nor was Jonathan Pritts anywhere in sight. My guards were restless, most of them men with families who wanted to be with them on a big day like this.

Ma and the boys came in about noon, Ma riding in the buckboard with Joe driving. Ollie had held a place for them where Ma could hear the speaking, and it would be the first time she had ever heard Orrin make a speech. Folks were mighty impressed with speech-making those days, and a man who could talk right up and make his words sound like something, well, he rated mighty high up there. He was a big man.

That day I was wearing black broadcloth pants down over my boots, a style just then coming in, and I had on a gray shirt with a black string tie and a black, braided Spanish-style jacket and a black hat. My gun was on, and I was carrying a spare tucked into my waistband out of sight under my jacket.

About noon Caribou Brown rode into town with Doubleout Sam. Shea saw them ride in and reported to me at once and I went down to the saloon where they had bellied up to the bar.

"All right, boys. Finish your drink and ride out."

They turned around on me, the both of them, but they knew me pretty well by then. "You're a hard man," Brown said. "Can't a man stay around for the fun?"

"Sorry."

They had their drinks but they didn't like it and when they finished them I was standing right there. "If you boys start right now you can make Vegas," I told them. "You'll have trouble if you think you can stay. I'll throw you both in jail and you'll be there next month at this time."

"On what charge?" Sam didn't like it.

"Loitering, obstructing justice, interfering with an officer, peddling without a license . . . I'll think of something."

"Oh, damn you!" Brown said. "Come on, Sam . . . let's ride."

They started for the door.

"Boys?"

They turned. "Don't circle around. I've got some deputies

who are mighty concerned about the town today. You're known men and if you come back they'll be shooting on sight."

They rode out of town and I was glad to see them go. Both were known trouble makers of the old Settlement crowd and they had been in several shootings.

The streets began to grow empty as folks drifted toward the speech-making and the band concert, which was going full blast. Going slow along the walks the streets were so empty the sound of my heels was loud. When I reached the adobe where Fetterson was held, I stopped by. Shea was on guard there.

"Hello, Fett," I said.

He got up and came to the bars. "That right? That they shot into my cell? Into a dummy?"

"What did you expect? You can hang him, Fetterson, and he knows that. He's got to do something . . . or run!"

Fetterson rubbed his jaw. The man looked worried. "How does a man get into these things?" he asked suddenly. "Damn it, I played square with him."

"He's wrong, Fett. He cares nothing for you except in so far as you are useful and when your usefulness is ended, so's his interest. You're too good a man to be wasted, Fett . . . you're loyal to a man who does not understand loyalty."

"Maybe . . . maybe."

He listened to the band, which was playing *My Darling Nelly Gray*. "Sounds like a good time," he said wistfully.

"I've got to go," I said, "the speaking starts in a few minutes."

He was still standing by the bars when I went out. Shea got up and walked outside with me. "Are you expecting trouble?"

"At any minute."

"All right," he cradled the shotgun in his arms, "I just don't want to miss all the fun."

From the gathering place beyond the buildings I could hear Ollie introducing somebody. Pausing, I listened. It was the speaker from Santa Fe—the one who preceded Orrin—and I could hear his rolling tones, although he was too far away to distinguish more than a word or two, and when it happened, it happened so suddenly that I was taken by surprise.

They came into the street below the jail and they came suddenly and they were on foot. Obviously they had been hidden during the night in the houses of some of the citizens, and there were eight of them and they had rifles. Everyone of them was a familiar face, all were from the old Settlement crowd, and they had me dead to rights.

149

They were near the jail and there was a man inside. There were probably two men inside. Up the street behind me Shea could do little unless I gave him room, but I had to be where I could do the most damage.

Turning at right angles I walked right into the middle of the street and then I faced them. Sixty yards separated us. Looking at those rifles and shotguns I knew I was in trouble and plenty of it, but I knew this was what I had been waiting for.

There were eight of them and they would be confident, but they would also be aware that I was going to get off at least one shot and probably one man would be killed . . . nobody would want to be that man.

"What are you boys getting out of this?" I asked them coolly. "Fifty dollars apiece? It's a cinch Jonathan isn't going to pay more than that . . . hope you collected in advance."

"We want the keys!" The man talking was named Stott. "Toss them over here!"

"You're talking, Stott . . . but are you watching? You boys are going to get it from the jail."

"The keys!"

Stott I was going to kill. He was the leader. I was going to get him and as many more as possible.

There was a rustle of movement down the street behind them. There was movement down there but I didn't dare take my eyes off them. So I started to walk. I started right down the street toward them, hoping to get so close they would endanger each other if they started shooting. Beyond them I could see movement and when I realized who it was I was so startled they might have killed me.

It was Dru.

She wasn't alone. She had six buckskin-clad riders with her and they all had Winchesters and they looked like they wanted to start shooting.

"All right," I said, "the fun's over. Drop your gun belts."

Stott was angry. "What are you trying—" Behind him seven Winchesters were cocked on signal, and he looked sharply around. And after that it was settled . . . they were not nearly so anxious for trouble and when they were disarmed, they were jailed along with the others.

Dru walked her horse up to the front of the jail. "Miguel saw them coming," she said, "so we rode down to help."

"Help? You did it all."

We talked there in the street and then I walked beside her horse over to the speaking. When this was over I was going to go after Jonathan Pritts. I was going to arrest him but oddly enough, I did not want him jailed. He was an old man, and defeat now would ruin him enough and he was whipped. When this was over he would be arrested, but if St. Vrain, Romero, and the others agreed, I'd just send him out of town with his daughter and a buckboard . . . they deserved each other.

Orrin was introduced. He got up and walked to the front of the platform and he started to speak in that fine Welsh voice of his. He spoke quietly, with none of that oratory they had been hearing. He just talked to them as he would to friends in his own home, yet as he continued his voice grew in power and conviction, and he was speaking as I had never heard him speak.

Standing there in the shade of a building I listened and was proud. This was my brother up there . . . this was Orrin. This was the boy I'd grown up with, left the mountains with, herded cattle, and fought Indians beside.

There was a strange power in him now that was born of thought and dream and that fine Welsh magic in his voice and mind. He was talking to them of what the country needed, of what had to be done, but he was using their own language, the language of the mountains, the desert, the cattle drives. And I was proud of him.

Turning away from the crowd, I walked slowly back to the street and between the buildings and when I emerged on the sunlit street, Tom Sunday was standing there.

I stopped where I stood and could not see his eyes but as flecks of light from the shadow beneath his hat brim.

He was big, broad, and powerful. He was unshaved and dirty, but never in my life had I seen such a figure of raw, physical power in one man.

"Hello, Tom."

"I've come for him, Tyrel. Stay out of the way."

"He's building his future," I said, "you helped him start it, Tom. He's going to be a big man and you helped him."

Maybe he didn't even hear me. He just looked at me straight on like a man staring down a narrow hallway.

"I'm going to kill him," he said, "I should have done it years ago."

We were talking now, like in a conversation, yet something warned me to be careful. What had Cap said? He was a killer and he would go on killing until something or somebody stopped him.

This was the man who had killed the Durango Kid, who had killed Ed Fry and Chico Cruz . . . Chico never even got off a shot.

"Get out of the way, Tye," he said, "I've nothing against you, I—"

He was going to kill me.

I was going to die . . . I was sure of it.

Only he must not come out of it alive. Orrin must have his future. Anyway, I was the mean one . . . I always had been.

Once before I had stepped in to help Orrin and I would now.

There was nobody there on the street but the two of us, just Tom Sunday, the man who had been my best friend, and me. He had stood up for me before this and we had drunk from the same rivers, fought Indians together. . . .

"Tom," I said, "remember that dusty afternoon on that hillside up there on the Purgatoire when we. . . ."

Sweat trickled down my spine and tasted salt on my lips. His shirt was open to his belt and I could see the hair on his big chest and the wide buckle of his belt. His hat was pulled low but there was no expression on his face.

This was Tom Sunday, my friend . . . only now he was a stranger.

"You can get out of the way, Tye," he said, "I'm going to kill him."

He spoke easily, quietly. I knew I had it to do, but this man had helped teach me to read, he had loaned me books, he had ridden the plains with me.

"You can't do it," I said. Right then, he went for his gun.

There was an instant before he drew when I knew he was going to draw. It was an instant only, a flickering instant that triggered my mind.

My hand dropped and I palmed my gun, but his came up and he was looking across it, his eyes like white fire, and I saw the gun blossom with a rose of flame and felt my own gun buck in my hand, and then I stepped forward and left—one quick step—and fired again.

He stood there looking across his gun at me and then he fired, but his bullet made a clean miss. Thumbing back the hammer I said, "Damn it, Tom. . . ." and I shot him in the chest.

He still stood there but his gun muzzle was lowering and he was still looking at me.

A strange, puzzled expression came into his eyes and he stepped toward me, dropping his gun. "Tyrel . . . Tye, what. . . ." He reached out a hand toward me, but when I stepped quickly to take it, he fell.

He went full face to the dust, falling hard, and when he hit the ground he groaned, then he half-turned and dropping to my knees I grabbed his hand and gripped it hard.

"Tye . . . Tye, damn it, I. . . ." He breathed hoarsely, and the front of his shirt was red with blood.

"The books," he whispered, "take the . . . books."

He died like that, gripping my hand, and when I looked up the street was full of people, and Orrin was there, and Dru.

And over the heads of some of the nearest, Jonathan Pritts.

Pushing through the crowd I stopped, facing Jonathan. "You get out of town," I told him, "you get out of the state. If you aren't out of town within the hour, or if you ever come back, for any reason at all, I'll kill you."

He just turned and walked away, his back stiff as a ramrod . . . but it wasn't even thirty minutes until he and Laura drove from town in a buckboard.

"That was my fight, Tye," Orrin said quietly, "it was my fight."

"No, it was mine. From the beginning it was mine. He knew it would be, I think. Maybe we both knew it . . . and Cap. I think Cap Rountree knew it first of all."

We live on the hill back of Mora, and sometimes in Santa Fe, Dru and me . . . we've sixty thousand acres of land in two states and a lot of cattle. Orrin, he's a state senator now, and pointing for greater things.

Sometimes of an evening I think of that, think when the shadows grow long of two boys who rode out of the high hill country of Tennessee to make a home in the western lands.

We found our home, and we graze and work our acres, and since that day in the street of Mora when I killed Tom Sunday I have never drawn a gun on any man.

Nor will I. . . .

A SELECTION OF FINE READING AVAILABLE IN CORGI BOOKS

Novels

☐ 552 08651 7   THE HAND REARED BOY   *Brian W. Aldiss* 35p
☐ 552 09018 2   A SOLDIER ERECT   *Brian W. Aldiss* 35p
☐ 552 07938 3   THE NAKED LUNCH   *William Burroughs* 45p
☐ 552 09090 5   THE LAST NIGHT OF SUMMER   *Erskine Caldwell* 30p
☐ 552 09104 9   CRY OF MORNING   *Brian Cleeve* 45p
☐ 552 09035 2   THE INVITATION   *Catherine Cookson* 35p
☐ 552 09074 3   LOVE AND MARY ANN   *Catherine Cookson* 30p
☐ 552 09076 X   MARRIAGE AND MARY ANN   *Catherine Cookson* 30p
☐ 552 08963 X   CAPE OF STORMS   *John Gordon Davis* 40p
☐ 552 08985 0   THE WELL OF LONELINESS   *Radclyffe Hall* 50p
☐ 552 09086 7   BLUE DREAMS   *William Hanley* 40p
☐ 552 09087 5   WHEN THE GALLOWS ARE HIGH   *Phyllis Hastings* 30p
☐ 552 08125 6   CATCH 22   *Joseph Heller* 40p
☐ 552 09051 4   THE ANALYST   *Alec Hilton* 35p
☐ 552 09033 6   WE SPEAK NO TREASON Vol 1   *Rosemary Hawley Jarman* 40p
☐ 552 09034 4   WE SPEAK NO TREASON Vol 2   *Rosemary Hawley Jarman* 40p
☐ 552 09019 0   THE CONCUBINE   *Norah Lofts* 35p
☐ 552 09105 7   HEAVEN IN YOUR HAND   *Norah Lofts* 35p
☐ 552 08791 2   HAWAII   *James A. Michener* 75p
☐ 552 09106 5   GODHEAD   *Paulo Montano* 35p
☐ 552 08124 8   LOLITA   *Vladimir Nabokov* 35p
☐ 552 07954 5   RUN FOR THE TREES   *James S. Rand* 40p
☐ 552 08887 0   VIVA RAMIREZ!   *James S. Rand* 40p
☐ 552 08930 3   STORY OF O   *Pauline Reage* 50p
☐ 552 08597 9   PORTNOY'S COMPLAINT   *Philip Roth* 40p
☐ 552 08945 1   THE HONEY BADGER   *Robert Ruark* 55p
☐ 552 08372 0   LAST EXIT TO BROOKLYN   *Hubert Selby Jr.* 50p
☐ 552 09050 6   PASSIONS OF THE MIND   *Irving Stone* 75p
☐ 552 09107 3   PASSIONATE JOURNEY   *Irving Stone* 40p
☐ 552 09108 1   BRAVE CAPTAINS   *Vivian Stuart* 30p
☐ 552 07807 7   VALLEY OF THE DOLLS   *Jacqueline Susann* 40p
☐ 552 08523 5   THE LOVE MACHINE   *Jacqueline Susann* 40p
☐ 552 08384 4   EXODUS   *Leon Uris* 50p
☐ 552 08866 6   QB VII   *Leon Uris* 50p
☐ 552 09109 X   SAFFRON AT THE COURT OF EDWARD III   *Julia Watson* 30p
☐ 552 08962 1   THE HELPERS   *Stanley Winchester* 40p
☐ 552 08481 6   FOREVER AMBER Vol. 1   *Kathleen Winsor* 40p
☐ 552 08482 4   FOREVER AMBER Vol. 2   *Kathleen Winsor* 40p

War

- [ ] 552 09042 5   **THE LUFTWAFFE WAR DIARIES**   *Cajas Becker* 60p
- [ ] 552 09055 7   **SIDESHOW**   *Gerald Bell* 30p
- [ ] 552 09041 7   **ALL STATIONS TO MALTA**   *Gilbert Hackforth-Jones* 30p
- [ ] 552 08874 9   **SS GENERAL**   *Sven Hassel* 35p
- [ ] 552 08779 3   **ASSIGNMENT GESTAPO**   *Sven Hassel* 35p
- [ ] 552 08855 2   **THE WILLING FLESH**   *Willi Heinrich* 35p
- [ ] 552 09110 3   **THE LOST COMMAND**   *Alastair Revie* 45p
- [ ] 552 08986 9   **DUEL OF EAGLES** (illustrated)   *Peter Townsend* 50p
- [ ] 552 08936 2   **JOHNNY GOT HIS GUN**   *Dalton Trumbo* 30p
- [ ] 552 09004 2   **THE LONG WATCH**   *Alan White* 25p
- [ ] 552 09092 1   **WEREWOLF**   *Charles Whiting* 35p

Romance

- [ ] 552 09099 9   **THE CORNER SHOP**   *Elizabeth Cadell* 25p
- [ ] 552 09043 3   **CANARY YELLOW**   *Elizabeth Cadell* 30p
- [ ] 552 09060 3   **SISTER CARLIN'S SUCCESSOR**   *Hilary Neal* 25p
- [ ] 552 09114 6   **HAD WE BUT WORLD ENOUGH AND TIME...** *Jean Ure* 25p

Science Fiction

- [ ] 552 09081 6   **STAR TREK 2**   *James Blish* 25p
- [ ] 552 08925 7   **THE BEST FROM NEW WRITINGS IN S.F.** ed. *John Carnell* 25p
- [ ] 552 09061 1   **LION OF COMARRE**   *Arthur C. Clarke* 30p
- [ ] 552 09115 4   **THE SHIP WHO SANG**   *Anne McCaffrey* 30p

General

- [ ] 552 09100 6   **FANNY HILL'S COOKBOOK**   *L. H. Braun & W. Adams* 40p
- [ ] 552 08926 5   **S IS FOR SEX**   *Robert Chartham* 50p
- [ ] 552 98958 4   **THE ISLAND RACE Vol. 1**   *Winston S. Churchill* 125p
- [ ] 552 98952 2   **THE ISLAND RACE Vol. 2**   *Winston S. Churchill* 125p
- [ ] 552 09011 5   **GEHLEN: SPY OF THE CENTURY** (illustrated)   *E. H. Cookridge* 50p
- [ ] 552 08800 5   **CHARIOTS OF THE GODS?** (illustrated) *Erich von Daniken* 35p
- [ ] 552 09073 2   **RETURN TO THE STARS**   *Erich von Daniken* 40p
- [ ] 552 07400 4   **MY LIFE AND LOVES**   *Frank Harris* 65p
- [ ] 552 98748 4   **MAKING LOVE** (Photographs)   *Walter Hartford* 85p
- [ ] 552 08992 3   **MASTERING WITCHCRAFT**   *Paul Huson* 35p
- [ ] 552 09062 X   **THE SENSUOUS MAN**   '*M*' 35p
- [ ] 552 08069 1   **THE OTHER VICTORIANS**   *Steven Marcus* 50p
- [ ] 552 09116 2   **A BRITISH SURVEY IN FEMALE SEXUALITY**   *Sandra McDermott* 40p
- [ ] 552 09030 1   **BORN TO HEAL** (illustrated)   *Paul Miller* 35p
- [ ] 552 08010 1   **THE NAKED APE**   *Desmond Morris* 30p
- [ ] 552 09044 1   **SEX ENERGY**   *Robert S. de Ropp* 35p
- [ ] 552 09016 6   **GOLF TACTICS**   *Arnold Palmer* 45p
- [ ] 552 08153 1   **MY GAME AND YOURS**   *Arnold Palmer* 50p
- [ ] 552 08880 3   **THE THIRTEENTH CANDLE**   *T. Lobsang Rampa* 35p
- [ ] 552 08974 5   **BRUCE TEGNER METHOD OF SELF DEFENCE**   40p
- [ ] 552 09059 X   **BEHIND THE MASK OF TUTANKHAMEN**   *Barry Wynne* 35p

Western

☐ 552 09095 6 APACHE *Will Levington Comfort* 30p

☐ 552 09113 8 TWO MILES TO THE BORDER No. 70 *J. T. Edson* 25p

☐ 552 08195 7 THE MAN FROM TEXAS No. 45 *J. T. Edson* 25p

☐ 552 09006 9 CALLAGHEN *Louis L'Amour* 30p

☐ 552 09058 1 RIDE THE DARK TRAIL *Louis L'Amour* 25p

☐ 552 09112 X THE DAYBREAKERS *Louis L'Amour* 25p

☐ 552 09048 4 RIO GRANDE No. 17 *Louis Masterson* 25p

☐ 552 09098 0 PAINTED PONIES *Alan Le May* 35p

☐ 552 09117 0 SUDDEN TAKES THE TRAIL *Oliver Strange* 25p

☐ 552 09096 4 ONLY THE VALIANT *Charles Marquis Warren* 35p

☐ 552 09093 X DEATH ON THE PRAIRIE *Paul I. Wellman* 30p

Crime

☐ 552 09077 8 THE BARON AT LARGE *John Creasey* 25p

☐ 552 09078 6 THE SECRET MURDER *John Creasey* 25p

☐ 552 09079 4 HUNT THE TOFF *John Creasey* 25p

☐ 552 08640 1 RED FILE FOR CALLAN *James Mitchell* 30p

☐ 552 08937 0 THE KNIVES OF JUSTICE *Mildred Savage* 50p

☐ 552 09056 5 SHAFT *Ernest Tidyman* 30p

☐ 552 09072 7 SHAFT'S BIG SCORE *Ernest Tidyman* 30p

All these book are available at your bookshop or newsagent: or can be ordered direct from the publisher. Just tick the titles you want and fill in the form below.

....

CORGI BOOKS, Cash Sales Department, P.O. Box 11, Falmouth, Cornwall.
Please send cheque or postal order. No currency, and allow 6p per book to cover the cost of postage and packing in the U.K., and overseas.

NAME ....

ADDRESS ....

(DEC. 72) ....